Make A Joyful Noise

An International Christmas Anthology

Introduction

I have had the pleasure of working with amazing and talented authors with this year's Christmas Anthology.

I am proud and happy with what we have accomplished together.

Make a Joyful Noise was a labor of love and brought joy into my life. We all hope that what is written within these pages does the same for you.

2020 has been a year filled with fear and uncertainties, loss and sadness. Through these dark days, we pray that *Make A Joyful Noise* will be a light in that darkness.

I want to thank these awesome authors and you, our faithful and supportive readers, for your love and support.

We wish you all a Merry Christmas and a Holiday Season filled to the brim with laughter, light, and love.

Sue Veryser-Duncan

Slappy Cat Communications LLC

Index

Olga Maughan

My name is Olga Maughan, originally from Dublin but moved to Cavan sixteen years ago. I retired three years ago at the age of 66 years and have to say loving all the time I have to write. I love to paint and do some cross stitch also. I will try my hand at any craft really, always keeping busy.

The short stories I have written {fiction} have been published in Woman's Way Magazine our leading mag here in Ireland.

So privileged to be taken on by them. I also have articles in the online magazine http://www.writing.ie in their mining memories section these are non-fiction. I have written a few novels but these are still sitting on my laptop.

REDICULOUS CHRISTMAS JUMPERS

By Olga Maughan

It was later than usual when I finished clearing the dinner dishes away; the kitchen was nice and tidy now, table set for breakfast in the morning. All I had to do was take out the garbage, then off to bed. It was a chilly night outside; a light frost had fallen. The skies were clear and all you could see was the twinkle of the stars. Such a stillness, I loved it, just perfect for this time of year. It was said we would have snow, but I think that was just wishful thinking. It was too cold, even for snow. I quickly opened the lid of the bin and was just about drop the bag in when I heard it. Low at first, then, as if desperate to be heard, it got louder. I moved the last bag I had put into the bin and there it was, a small grey cat, it had somehow got stuck in my bin. I reached inside to help her out, believing I was going to get scratched by claws. What could I do? I couldn't leave her there. She allowed me to lift her, no scratching no hissing, it was as if she knew I meant no harm. I placed her on the ground, shooed her gently away. She stood there, looking at me pleadingly, I knew she must be hungry. How long had she been in there? It was two days since I last dropped garbage into the bin. I did what I told my son Sam and husband Alan never to do, I brought her out food and a saucer of milk. No harm I thought, she will go home now, they would be none the wiser.

I woke with the alarm the next morning, Alan, still asleep. The alarm for him went unheard. I could hear Sam in his room, awake, playing with his cars. It would take Alan at least another twenty minutes before he woke properly. I always left him there, as I and Sam would get ready first, and then he would help me with breakfast. I popped my head around Sam's door. "Good morning mum" I kissed his head. "Mum, I heard a cat, it woke me up, can I have a cat for Christmas? Can I mum? Can I?" I smiled at him, as I remembered last night, I only hope that the cat had gone home. I hoped it wasn't down in the bins again. "I don't think Santa would bring animals for Christmas," I said. Thinking about the cat I regretted now that I had fed her.

At the breakfast table, Sam told Alan all about the cat that woke him; In between mouthful of cornflakes, he said how he would love a cat for Christmas. Alan reminded him about his friend Thomas, he got a dog last year, "do you remember Sam? how his mum had to send it back to Santa because she couldn't cope with the mess he made, and how poor Thomas was so upset about losing his pet?" Sam flopped back in his chair. A face, so forlorn, it would make you give in to his requests. Alan looked at me knowingly, he knew what I was thinking, what harm would a little kitten do? he shook his head and smiled. We said nothing, soon hunger got the better of Sam and he continued to eat.

When I came home from dropping Sam at school I turned on the Christmas tree lights, they were perfect. The room looked lovely all ready for Santa's visit. I prepared a chicken casserole for the evening dinner. I popped it into the oven. After I tidied up, I sat in the kitchen with a cuppa, the kitchen, so lovely and warm now from the heat of the oven.

I heard it again. I opened the door to make sure. She ran past me, over to stove where she too felt the warmth of the oven. Mistake number two, I fed her again. How could I not.? She looked so cold and, as small as she was, she had a big tummy. I feared the worse. Alan would be cross; he would expect me to bring her somewhere so a home could be found for her. She slept by the stove, enjoying all the heat on such a cold winter day. I sat in the kitchen, listening to the radio while she purred. It made me feel relaxed just to listen to her. An hour later she wanted out. I never saw her again that day or night. I hoped she had found her way home. I hated to think of her out in all weathers, and if I was right, she would have kittens soon. I scolded myself for not bringing her to our Vet. He might have found her a home or at least kept her until after Christmas.

It was Christmas Eve and everything was ready for Santa's visit. Sam was asleep this past two hours, it had taken an hour to convince him he needed to get his rest before tomorrow. Alan went out to the bins to get rid of the remains of wrapping paper. We would head to bed early; we were sure we would be up at the crack of dawn with one excited child. As Alan came towards the back door I thought I saw something out of the corner of my eye. I hoped it wasn't the cat. Alan would know by her behavior that it wasn't the first time she had been in our kitchen. When I turned there was no sign of her. Must have been my imagination. I felt glad, but guilty at the same time that I was unable to give her a Christmas treat, which I'm sure she needed as I was convinced she was about to have kittens.

Alan was ready for bed, I told him I would be up later, "just a few more bits to see to before I join you, won't belong." Alan knew well enough what I was about to do, I don't know why I did it behind his back, but I did it every year since Sam was born. I always bought Alan a Christmas jumper, an extra present, just for fun, to put under the tree. It had become a standing joke in the family now. Alan hated them, but always went along with it for Sam's sake. He loved his dad's Christmas jumpers and was just as excited to see what was on the front of the jumper as he was about his own presents. I looked back at the tree and was pleased with this year's effort, it all looked very festive.

No alarm was needed in our house that Christmas morning. Sam was up and jumping for joy. He could hardly wait to get downstairs, as he bounced on our bed and pleaded with his dad to wake up. Alan teased him, "oh my eyes are so tired they won't open, what can I do?" they both tumbled around for a few seconds, and went downstairs, Sam on his dad's back, me close on their heels. Sam opened the door, and there, by the tree, where most of the toys he had asked for sat waiting for him to open. It all looked beautiful. Sam's face glowed with excitement. But as I looked closer I knew at

once that some of the presents I had bought Alan had been moved. Sam and Alan went down on their knees to get a closer look, and there was that sound again. "Meow" and a long purr. She had slipped past both of us last night. I hadn't imagined it after all.

She had made a bed out of Alan's Christmas jumper that I so carefully wrapped last night, the paper was in tatters, the jumper unwearable. Sam squealed in delight. "Daddy Santa brought us a cat for Christmas, a few cats, I love Santa" Sam lay on his tummy talking to the little grey cat, telling her how much he loved her and how he would take care of her. Yes, there she was, my little grey cat, looking so pleased with herself. Turning on her back to show off her three babies who looked just like herself.

Then poor Sam, looking so alarmed, said, "dad, the cat made a bed from your jumper, what will you wear now?" Poor Sam, he turned from delight to worrying about his dad's jumper. Alan took him in his arms. He was smiling, it had only dawned on him, for the first Christmas since we married he would not have to wear a "Ridiculous Christmas Jumper" as he called them. Don't worry Sam, it's ok, I can wear a normal jumper this year. My little cat curled herself around her babies just then and snuggled into the reindeer's head that was on the front of Alan's Christmas jumper, looking very pleased with herself. I believe she won Alan's heart there and then. Having saved him from having to put his "ridiculous jumper" on for the day, but what would he really have to say about the little grey cat.? Without looking at Alan I knew he was eying me questionably. I dared to turn, looked at him, and shrugged.

Sam and I were over the moon about the unexpected Santa gift. We spent more time that day looking at the little grey cat and her three kittens than we did admiring our Christmas gifts. Whatever about Alan's ridiculous jumper, this little grey cat and her kittens were one Christmas present that would never be returned.

Not if Sam and I had anything to do with it.

ICE CREAM IN WINTER

By Olga Maughan

I stood at the window watching for them to arrive, looking back at the table I had set for the evening meal and wondering if I had perhaps made a mistake. Ice cream dishes? in weather like this?

Surely, they would prefer something warmer. *They're no longer children,* my husband Tony had said. There was a time when nothing, but ice cream would do, no matter what the weather was doing outside. It was their favourite, even on Christmas day.

As always, I went to the trouble of making all sorts of desserts for Christmas day, Trifle, Christmas pudding with all the trimmings, fresh fruit salad sitting in scooped out pineapple skins topped with cream and cherries on top. I can still hear their little voices as I tried to tempt them with beautiful desserts, I had spent hours preparing, *no mum, we don't want any of those, ice cream please, only ice cream.* How I loved those years when my girls Vera and Ann were small, everything was magical.

The first sound on Christmas morning, their voices calling me and their dad to wake up and see what Father Christmas had brought them. We were awake of course, long before they were, just as excited to see their little faces light up when we walked into the room to see what was under the tree. They were never disappointed, good girls who really appreciated everything they were given. Their only complaint would have been if I had forgotten the ice cream.

I went to check on the oven, if they didn't arrive soon the steak and kidney pie would be ruined, I covered the roast potatoes, the vegetables were fine, cooked already only to be heated through. I looked at the freshly baked mince pies, perhaps I could make custard and serve those instead of ice cream. Yes, that would do.

My girls Ann and Vera were coming home with their husbands to spend Christmas with us, they both lived on the other side of the world and didn't get home very often. My fear of flying kept me grounded so I had never been to visit their homes. Thank goodness for facetime on Whats App, at least I could see their homes. And the grandchildren, how I wished I could hug them and not just see them on a screen.

It was seven years since the two of them had been home together. They had come with their husbands back then and only one grandchild, now they had five between them. Ann was the eldest and had two boys, Vera a year younger had two girls and her last child was a boy. I would have eleven to cater for on Christmas day. Well, ten, the youngest grandchild was only six months old. I was so looking forward to their arrival with all the little people I was going to get to know properly for the first time. I wished with all my heart they were still living at home.

I realised how much I was missing not having my grandchildren close but guarantees of better jobs for their husbands took them away. I could hardly blame them, if I had to do it all over again, I might just do the same, or maybe not.

I was always a home bird, never wanted to fly, always believing something dreadful would happen. My long-suffering husband, Tony, was so patient with me and would never push me to go anywhere I didn't want to. I did fly, of course I did, when we went on honeymoon to Greece and if I had refused Tony said he would have gone without me. At the time he really didn't understand just how much of an ordeal it was for me. We went away a few times when the children were young but when Tony saw how bad a reaction those wonderful holidays had on me, we holidayed at home from then on and were just as happy exploring our own country.

I looked out the window again, a light sprinkling of snow had started to fall to add to the much larger downfall earlier this morning. A White Christmas was so perfect. I strained to see if the cars were coming. Tony had gone to the airport, even though they were hiring cars when they landed, he felt it was only right to be there to greet his beloved daughters. I knew the real reason why he went; he wanted to leave me to the food preparation, he knew I would be fussing over the meal and wondering if I had done enough of everything. No matter how hard he tried to help I would always feel I needed to do it myself.

His voice echoed in my head as I took the custard I had prepared for the mince pies off the heat, *you do far too much as usual Jane, you know we will never get through all that, there's enough to feed an army.*

And that's what I thought I was doing, eleven mouths to feed; I don't think I ever had such a busy Christmas as this one. Still, it won't go to waste, tomorrow is Christmas eve, we can reheat any food leftover for lunch. I checked the table once again, making sure I had enough places set. The ice cream dishes were so old but still retained their vibrant colours, a beautiful painting of red strawberries and dark blueberries with a very lovely green on the leaf of the fruit and a pink scoop of ice cream, a hint of summer on what was going to be a cold Christmas. The snow was falling hard now.

I could hear them before I saw them, I rushed to the door. Hugs, kisses, and lots of tears before they got children and luggage into the house and out of the blustery snowfall. I was overjoyed to have them all here. I couldn't get enough hugs from those wonderful grandchildren. The poor little mites staring at me wondering why their grandmother cried every time she looked at them.

Something smells delicious Vera said, as we made our way into the dining room. Both Vera and Ann laughed as they took in the dining table and spotted the dishes that were part of their childhood. *See,* they said, almost in unison to their husbands and children, "*we told you there would be ice cream, no matter how cold it is outside always ice cream in winter. What would Christmas day be if we didn't have a scoop of ice cream as an option for dessert? The grandchildren clapped their hands with delight, they take after us Vera said, they love their ice cream too. Can't get enough of it.*

She hugged me, *come on mum, I'll help you serve up dinner."*

Tony smiled at me and gave me a knowing wink as if it was all his idea and he hadn't told me not to be a silly old woman and put the ice cream dishes away. *Old habits die hard,* I said, a tradition I knew would be carried on for many more Christmas's to come.

ROBIN   *By Olga Maughan*

I watched you in spring as you made

your nest

in the tree root

disturbed, you moved, you and your mate

to what was left of the winter log pile

coming and going to feed your clutch

Singing together, defending your territory

all summer

I spied you on the garden fence

Puffing out your body

as you shook the light fall of snow

from your feathers

My little robin, my little friend

Although I see you all year round

It's Christmas when you're at your best

I listen for your song,

the dawn chorus you start

the last to stop

How many clutches did you have this year?

Now all alone, except for me

I will feed you fruit and nuts

To keep you safe from winters shortfall

and meager offerings

the ground too hard to peck for worms

Rest now December is here

your song silent

till Christmas passes

© Olga

"I left Santa gluten-free cookies and organic soy milk and he put a solar panel in my stocking."

– Unknown

Amazing Peace

"We clap hands and welcome the Peace of Christmas. We beckon this good season to wait a while with us."

--Maya Angelou

"Anyone who believes that men are the equal of women has never seen a man trying to wrap a Christmas present."

– Unknown

Alan Dean Naldret

I was lucky enough to have met Alan, a few years back while doing book signings together. He also wrote history pieces for my newspaper, The Beacon NewsMagazine.

When I asked Alan if he would like to write a story for this year's Christmas Anthology, he was so excited that he sent in his story in August. And he thanked me for the opportunity.

The honor was all mine.

Alan passed away on September 3, 2020. He was an amazing historian, author, teacher, and friend. He will be missed by the many lives he touched

Alan's joy, love, and laughter will never be forgotten.

God Bless you, my friend.

May the Dear Lord hold you in the palm of His hand.

God's Speed, Alan. Until we meet again.

The Place in Michigan
Where It is Always Christmas

By Alan Dean Naldret

The residents of Christmas, Michigan in the Upper Peninsula like Christmas a lot. Of course, who doesn't? However, the Christmas residents of Michigan just might like the holiday a bit *more* than most, since it clearly drives the local economy and it is the only place in Michigan where it's ALWAYS Christmas!

Christmas, Michigan was just a swampy area at first; near a ghost town named Onota, which was an iron smelting town that burned down in 1877, leaving only the ruins of an iron kiln. Since the whole town's economy was based on the furnace that closed, once the town burned and the furnace closed, the whole town emptied—until it could come up with something else to base the town's whole economy on. The area being declared a historic area named Bay Furnace didn't solve the low population problem.

It took over seventy years for the area to find a new industry. The whole area was bought and named "Christmas" by game warden Julius Thorson in 1938. He came from nearby Munising. Thorson started a toy factory in this isolated area to make holiday gifts. However, this town's purpose was lost less than two years later when the gift factory burned down in June 1940. One of the Thorson girls living there discovered the fire and managed to alert everyone and save them so that there were no fatalities. But the factory was never rebuilt.

In spite of the toy factory burning down, the town still retained the name. As residents moved in and built summer homes, they got into the spirit of the town and gave their streets Christmas holiday names, including St. Nicholas Street, Sleigh Way, Jingle Bells Road, Evergreen, Santa Way, and more.

The town received new fame in 1966 when it was given a post office. Its new purpose was to have people from all over the United States pay extra to have their Christmas mail sent to and from the Alger County community and postmarked from there with the desired "Christmas" postmark.

The famous Christmas postmark

Long-time Christmas town entrance sign, which was unfortunately recently removed.

(Below) A 35-foot tall Santa Claus standing next to a giant pole that has "North Pole" written on it is one of the most well-known features of Christmas, Michigan,

Christmas postmark stamping is often done at the Christmas Mall of Joe and Karen Beauchaines. The official Christmas zip code is 49862. The Munising Post Office sends their Christmas mail to the Beauchaines, who often hand-stamp them, with their son Brady and loyal employee Katie helping out. They do it at the Christmas Mall, the gift shop they purchased in 1995. To all of them, it is a labor of love. By 2002, they were stamping over 20,000 items for free each year! That is definitely getting into the Christmas spirit!

With the Pictured Rocks, Bay Furnace Rustic Campground, and Hiawatha Forest nearby, the Christmas area continues to thrive as a tourist area, both winter and summer. (Not to mention it has a very popular hunting season in the autumn also.) It now has 400 full-time residents and many part-time summer inhabitants who come for the mild temperatures. It's so mild that Christmas once had snow in July!

Other summer attractions include many new resorts, campgrounds, and golf courses, where visitors can enjoy swimming, fishing, kayaking, hiking, canoeing, boating, scuba diving, snorkeling, or even just plain relaxing! Great places to hike to are some of the many beautiful waterfalls in the area. Other summer choices include camping, horseback riding, biking, water-skiing, and more.

But winter businesses are probably the most well-known. Snowmobile businesses are starting to get big. Other businesses with Christmas themes continue to do well! These include skiing, including cross-country skiing, snow-shoeing, snowmobile racing, ice golfing, ice skating, snow sledding, snow tubing, ice-climbing, and fat-tire biking. You can even visit frozen waterfalls!

Lodging choices include not only the Christmas Motel, but Christmas Paradise, Evergreen Cottage, Winter Dreamland, and the Yule Log Resort.

What's a resort area in the Upper Peninsula without a lighthouse? Well, Christmas has one known as the Grand Island West Channel Rear Range Light (try saying that five times fast!). It is also called the End of the Road Lighthouse. And it still operates, guiding boats around Grand Island and into the harbor of Munising. A rumor is that a local landowner tried to introduce some new animal species into the area. When he found

out the lighthouse keeper was hunting his newly-placed animals for food, he had a bounty put on the lighthouse keeper's head!

The Grand Island West Channel Rear Range Light

Santa's Workshop in Christmas, Michigan

See Next Page

The Christmas Motel

By Alan Dean Naldret

Michigan has many other towns that celebrate Christmas but not to the extent of Christmas, Michigan. There is Frankenmuth, Michigan, which has Bronner's, said by many to be the largest Christmas store in the world, with over 90,000 square feet of shopping space. That is almost the size of two football fields. They carry over 50,000 varieties of Christmas trims, gifts, and collectibles!

Detroit, Grand Rapids, Holland with their Parade of Lights, Rochester, Traverse City, Dearborn, with Christmas in Greenfield Village, and Mackinac Island are all well-known for their Christmas décor and decorations. But Christmas, Michigan, with all of its Christmas themed businesses and décor, and a multitude of winter sports has them all beat.

What more could a winter resort have that Christmas doesn't? How about a casino? Christmas now has the Kewadin Casino. Now you can celebrate Christmas with a game of blackjack or some slots!

Christmas, Michigan, is just one of at least eight towns in the United States named Christmas, as well as others named with Christmas themes such as Noel, North Pole, Mistletoe, Bethlehem, and Santa Claus. There are towns with the actual name of Christmas in Arizona, Florida, Kentucky, Mississippi, Maine, Oregon, Utah, and Tennessee. But the Christmas in Michigan might just be the one that enjoys it the most!. However, the majority of residents of Christmas don't get into the spirit as much as the resident, who, after a night of hard partying, attempted to enter his home via the chimney and had to be rescued by the local fire department.

Have a Merry Christmas!

Barbie-Jo Smith

Barbie-Jo Smith is a natural storyteller and author of 5 books. An award-winning writer and poet, selections of her work appear in 33 anthologies from Canada and the United States. Some of her writing genres include, cowboy story poems, humorous short stories, and a cookbook.

Most recently, she's working on a children's book series and romantic murder mystery.

Our Country Christmas Tree

By Barbie-Jo Smith

It was Saturday, two weeks before Christmas and parents, Pete and Jane, were enjoying a cup of coffee. Pete had found an advertisement from the newspaper featuring Christmas trees for $2.00 each. All you had to do was drive to the country and cut them. Pretty easy stuff, he concluded. Several cups of strong coffee made the idea seem irresistible to him; however, Jane heard alarm bells going off in her head. Peter reported that it was time they experienced the wonder of going for their own tree and, besides, wouldn't it be lots of fun to go out for a relaxing family day in the country. The children, Michael and Michelle, needed to learn that the Yuletide tree didn't necessarily have to come from a box or from the Cub and Scout lot. Anyway, the price was right. More alarm bells for Jane. Pete rationalized that because their living room ceiling was slanted and 12 feet high at the top end, a nice big scotch pine would be wonderful snuggled into one of the corners. There was obviously no way that Jane could dissuade him from his quest, so she quietly suggested that he take the children and the dog and have a nice day. She would keep the home fires burning and have a nice warm stew waiting for them on their return. Jane was a very smart woman!

The advertisement said there would be a bonfire burning if people wanted to bring hot chocolate and wieners to make it a wonderful Yuletide family experience. Just drive northwest out of the city, turn on the gravel road, and follow the signs. It was only "about a ½ hour" drive. Knowing that Pete's talents did not include planning, Jane ensured that her children were properly dressed in snowsuits, with boots, mittens, hats, and scarves. The dog, Star wagged her tail in anticipation, so a quick executive decision was made. The travel group became one adult, two children, and one hairy dog.

Meanwhile, the limit of Pete's planning was to throw rope into the trunk of the car. One rope was good and two ropes were better. He had an idea that he would also cut a tree for their good friends, Stan and Wendy, who had a young family just like them. They would be so surprised and delighted. This was going to be fun!

Although the family had two cars, one a large station wagon, Pete chose to take the small compact car. He calculated their gas savings with glee. A $2.00 Christmas tree and good gas mileage. Of course, he forgot that the roof rack was on the big car and also the size of the car as it related to the trees. Well, at least, he had lots of rope. It never occurred to him to check the weather or depth of snow. The little car steamed northward and exited on the gravel road as planned. There were other cars headed in the same direction, so Pete just followed along. The road became progressively rougher as they advanced and they had to slow down to cross some sunken culverts. Presently, they crossed the last culvert, dodged some rather large holes in the frozen gravel, and drove into a meadow. The bonfire crackled cheerily and cars were parked to the sides. What a beautiful place. There were hills and valleys just filled with trees from which to choose.

They decided to split up and go in different directions to scout out the best trees. Michelle took Star on her leash, Michael went off on another trail, and Pete headed forward. Of course, the minimal planning phase didn't include proper clothing for Pete. He stepped off the parking lot into foot deep snow. He was wearing running shoes, jeans, a short bomber jacket, and ancient ski mittens. He didn't have a hat and carried only a hatchet, having forgotten the saw at home.

Eventually, they found three suitable trees, agreed on one, and Pete went to work while the children played with the dog. It wasn't a Scotch pine, but it was a really nice, tall tree with lots of branches and good shape. Because the branches were growing all the way to the ground, Pete had to first clear away a lot of snow to get access to the trunk. Then he knelt down in the snow to begin hacking. He muttered to himself that he should have brought the saw, but this was all he had, and weren't they all having fun in the country.

The children were completely ignoring him and having a wonderful time rolling and playing in the snow with each other and the dog. The dog was in heaven as she bounded around, plunging her head into the soft snow, and then jumping out again. Every once in awhile, she had to stop and lay down to nibble the ice chunks out from between her toes. Then she was at it again. They were having a grand time.

Meanwhile, Pete was now laying on his side with the snow melting on his bare back as the bomber jacket slipped up. It didn't take long for his jeans to get damp and, of course, his feet had long since lost their feeling. He felt as if he had two blocks of wood on the ends of his shins. He realized he was very cold; however, he persevered and managed to cut through the trunk. With a call of timber, the tree sank onto its side.

Because Pete was so cold, the tree for their friends was chosen quickly. It wasn't quite as regal as the one they chose for themselves, but it was acceptable and would fit in Stan and Wendy's living room. There were some bare spots, but Pete rationalized that a few extra strands of tinsel would quickly fix up that problem. In no time, he had the second tree cut and realized the downside of the beautiful hills. He manhandled the trees over several hills and valleys, and eventually back to the car. The children and dog frolicked beside him. They were as warm as toast and oblivious to their father's predicament. Pete thought how good hot chocolate and hot dogs would taste and with a sinking feeling remembered exactly where they were—at home on the counter. With a resigned sigh, he clomped along on his block-like feet.

 Pete loaded the kids in the car, followed by Star whose coat was so puffed out from snow between the hairs that she looked like a small pony. As the car warmed up, the snow melted, and the smell was akin to having a wet sheep in the vicinity. Pete looked at the size of the trees. They seemed small growing in the forest, but here beside the car, they were huge. Thank goodness he had an extra pile of rope. He knew there would be some lashing to the car, but he really did himself proud that day. He cracked the windows of the car, placed the trees on the car roof. Thank goodness he checked before tying them down because they were so long they completely covered the windshield. So, Peter reversed one of them making a sightline. He then lashed them to the car by running the ropes through the car and around the trees. With other ropes, he tied off the front and rear bumpers. Then he crawled into the car through the window, started the engine, and turned the heat up full blast. He then knew that particular agony when one's toes are warming up from being so cold, but oh, the heat in the car felt so good. Steam began to rise as his clothing thawed and they were quite a sight as they prepared to leave.

Pete was prudent as they left the parking lot and proceeded over the first sunken culvert. There was absolutely no load shift so all was very well to make the drive along the gravel road to the pavement. The drive home was uneventful, except for the rising steam and smell like they were all in a sheep shearing shed!

On their arrival home, the children ran to their mother, dog close behind, to tell her about all the fun they had. Dad must have had fun, too, because he had been laying in the snow playing with the hatchet and the tree! Pete untied the trees and chugged up the sidewalk, depositing them on the back deck. It was time to have a hot cup of coffee and change into dry clothes while his feet thawed.

While Pete and the kids were away, Jane re-arranged the living room to make room for the tree in the corner. Having thawed sufficiently to walk, Pete dragged their tree into the living room and in short order discovered that it was enormous, even with the high ceiling. He laid it down and cut about 2 feet off the bottom to fit it into the corner. This time the job was done with a saw. As Pete sawed away in the living room, Jane and the kids disappeared into the bowels of the basement to retrieve boxes of Christmas decorations.

Having shortened the tree to fit, Pete wrestled it into the tree stand to let it thaw, congratulating himself on such a grand find. He was especially happy that the tree was so fresh and wouldn't drop many needles. This was because so many needles were blown off during the drive home. Jane's delicious warm stew was served for supper and the whole family dug in as if they hadn't eaten for days. This was close to the truth because of the forgotten hot dogs.

After supper, when the tree had thawed and relaxed, it had to be positioned into the corner to camouflage the flaws. There were several gaping holes. As the children planned the decorating, Pete put the bulbs in miles of light strings. As lights were at that time, if one bulb was not working, the whole string didn't work; therefore, the light check could take ages. However, having patched everything together, Pete's next job was to deposit the lights on the top two-thirds of the tree, followed by the angel at the top. Being the tallest member of the family, the job naturally fell to him. As well, it's a time-honoured tradition that the father of the family strings the lights, plugging them in for the first time to make sure they're safe. If they're not, then he's subsequently blown off the ladder. It was thought that the tallest and strongest person in the family should have this job in order to survive the possible short circuits. With only a 6 foot ladder, Pete stretched to his full height to place the angel on the top. Then he threw the switch and the tree lit up with wonderful colour. The entire family stepped back to adore the huge deep green tree, the smell of spruce filling the room.

No time to waste, the children were hard at it putting decorations on the tree, especially into the bare spots. One bare spot might house a dozen ornaments and a pound of tinsel. First, came the ornaments, which were pulled out with awe as everyone remembered them from the year before. Then, came the garland followed by the tinsel. Finally, the coup de grace—candy canes. The children deposited them at a height they could easily reach if there was a candy emergency, but not low enough for the dog to reach. Too many times they had dealt with a dog that had intestinal difficulties at this time of year. When they finally realized that the dog was helping herself to peppermint candy, they moved it up a few branches, and the mystery illness disappeared.

After reaching all the high spots, Pete relaxed on the sofa to watch, a glass of Christmas cheer in his hand. All was right with his world. Despite a few hitches, the sojourn to the country to give the children a real country Christmas tree had gone surprisingly well. The feeling was returning to his feet and the chopping hadn't claimed any fingers. It had been a good adventure.

A few days later, Stan and Wendy stopped by and were apprized that their $2.00 tree was waiting for them on the deck. One look at the tree and their faces revealed that this poor tree with all the gaps and gouges was not quite suitable. They tactfully mentioned that they had already bought a tree. The second tree spent the Christmas season propped up on the deck in a way that it actually looked like it was growing there.

After the Christmas break, the children returned to school and Pete returned to work. The tree remained in the house until mid-January when it was decided that everyone was sick of looking at it. The Christmas season was definitely over. It was time to take it down and pack away the ornaments. The kids, having completely lost interest, promptly disappeared. Jane and Pete packed away the ornaments, tinsel, garland, and several pounds of candy canes.

Pete grappled with the tree and fought his way out the door, literally throwing it on the snow. He had long ago learned to drag the tree out backwards, having been unceremoniously impaled the first time he removed a real tree. Used trees could be taken to the local fire hall for disposal. This time Pete tied the tree to the roof rack on the big car. He also threw on the gift tree which, by now, was just a bare pole surrounded by a circular pile of needles. There was a huge pile of trees at the fire hall, some of which were still festooned with gaily coloured decorations. This was no doubt a testament from other fathers who had been commissioned to get rid of their trees.

One Saturday in August of that year, Jane and Pete sat over morning coffee reminiscing about Christmas and how much fun it was to have a real tree. Wasn't it beautiful and it really wasn't that hard to chop one down—was it?

Shortly after that, they went to a sale at the hardware store and bought a tree in a box.

Fran Porter

I am a retired English teacher and curriculum writer living with my husband, a retired geologist, in beautiful Calgary, Alberta, Canada. I have taught Creative Writing, done professional editing, and contributed to literary journals and magazines. One of my greatest loves (besides my husband, family, and friends!) is the reading and writing of well-crafted stories depicting compelling characters whose lives are changed forever as a result of those stories' events.

My first book, *When the Ship has no Stabilizers* (Crossfield Publishing, 2014) chronicled our younger daughter Colleen's battle with borderline personality disorder, a crippling mental illness. Proceeds from its sales totaled nearly $50,000 and were donated to McMan Youth, Family, and Community Services here in Calgary, for the opening of a free, no-waiting clinic on their premises for mentally ill adolescents. Proceeds from ongoing sales continue to support this clinic and have resulted –to our humble gratitude—in our being named 'Calgary 2017 Philanthropic Family of the Year.

My second book, *The Wrong Brother* (Crossfield Publishing, 2019) is a romantic suspense novel set in the fictitious Canadian Rockies town of Barrett, and is the first of a planned series, all taking place in that town. (*Dastardly Deed*, my second 'Barrett' novel, is with the publisher now, and I am well into a third.) For information about *The Wrong Brother*—published in 2019 and fourth on the local bestseller list following its launch, go to http://open-book.ca/News/Perspective-is-Everything!-Fran-L.-Porter-on-Crafting-Characters-Writing-Effective-Dialogue-More where I was a featured author that year on the Ontario literary site 'Open Book'.

My love of writing will remain with me forever, and I am proud to contribute a short story to your Christmas anthology. Thank you for including me!

Baggage

By Fran L. Porter

It was my first visit to Ruth at the retirement home since The Terrible Event. I don't mean the Parkinson's diagnosis that makes my dear friend's eyes so bleary and causes those exhausting involuntary tics. I mean the heinous act, two months before, of a callously practical daughter and son-in-law. "Phil and I did a great downsizing job! We threw out or gave away all Mom's rubble collected over the years," Vera had exulted. "There's just no room in her nice new place for so much junk, right?"

Junk? Those memorabilia were pieces of Ruth's life: reminders of travels with Nick before he'd passed, of milestones like the arrival of grandchildren or the Volunteer-of-the-Year award presented to her by the PTA. *Junk*? In mute anger, I'd nodded with the woodenness of a Bobblehead doll. After all, this was a family matter, and really none of my business. But I'd raged with agony and   pity for Ruth ever since. Being burdened, at her age, with the baggage of resentment and bitterness toward people who had wrested all control and independence from her had to be the epitome of injustice.

I set down the standard Christmas cookie platter from our church's Congregational Care Team on the front desk of the spacious lobby area in her building; then I held my hands under an automatic sanitizer dispenser and rubbed them together so briskly they stung. Yes, I *was* buying time. Yes, I *was* mentally assuming my friend's identity, vicariously basking in her pain. No, I *didn't* really want to be invited into the prison-cell sterility of her present living quarters, its scaled-down dimensions no doubt reducing what was once a charismatic dynamo of feminine feistiness to an empty shell of virtual nonentity. The cruelty of it didn't bear contemplating.

We'd been chums since girlhood, over seventy years. We'd skinned our knees on the playground together, done our nails in zany colours and patterns together, giggled over cute boys together, got drunk and sick for the first time together—and ultimately met the demon of encroaching old age together, with a never-say-die smirk and the clap of our gnarled fingers against one another's palms in a rebellious high-five. Tough pirates like us would weather the tempests of the world's high seas with perpetual bravery, we bragged, raising our wine glasses in a triumphant toast.

Ironically, it wasn't the high seas that got us in the end. It was that enemy pirate named Parkinson's, the one that gradually erodes both body and mind—the one ruthlessly robbing me of a pal closer to me than my own sister. The unfairness of it galled so much I could taste its acerbic bitterness on my tongue. Such a gobsmack simply hadn't been on our life's agenda. And part of me wished that paying Ruth this Christmas-cookie-delivery visit, in her illness-ravaged state, wasn't on my present life's agenda either.

But my day's mission had been determined. Congregational Care had unquestioningly put Ruth's name on my assigned list of cookie recipients, knowing of the longstanding bond between us. There was no shirking it. Turning right at the desk and proceeding about halfway down a long hallway to a curlicue-lettered unit on my left labeled 'Ruth Spencer', I gave the freshly-painted, robin-egg-blue door three staccato raps—our mutual signal since we were kids. Those raps meant I could turn the knob and enter—like family—without waiting on her permission.

"Flo! It's you! At last!" She rose from a couch just beyond the entranceway and came toward me, arms outstretched. Her still-lovely angelic face with its halo of ash-blonde hair lit with joy as we exchanged hugs. "So wonderful to see you—*and* the cookies! Why did you wait so long to visit? Come in and let me show you around!"

Bracing myself and still stalling, I handed her the plate I'd placed on the floor at my feet, and then I fussed with the business of shedding my outdoor shoes. Who can blame me, said my internal voice, for not wanting to witness how a whole lifetime can be so pathetically minimized? I began to mouth token compliments as she took my hand and led me from room to room, not really absorbing what I was being shown. But then something truly remarkable happened. Suddenly—and amazingly—I was infused with the wondrous spirit that is the essence of the season. And in my mind and heart, a bona fide Christmas miracle occurred.

For the first time in two months, I stopped wallowing in my own indignant misery. And what I *started* doing, at that same moment, was actually *listening* to Ruth.

"Don't you love this cozy quilt on the bed? Vera bought it for me at a craft fair! Look how it picks up the colours of the frame in that dresser photo of me and Nick in Nairobi, and in the plaque on my PTA award! Vera and Phil have been outstanding! They've helped me sort between essential and expendable, and they've set up a beautiful little nest for me here! It's such a modern, cheery unit, so welcoming! You know something? I'm finding that a person is never too old to let go of some of the past's clutter—just the *clutter*, mind you—and embrace whatever new experiences the future still holds."

An empty shell of virtual nonentity? Whatever blunderbuss of a fool had I been even to go down that road where my friend was concerned! Once more I nodded, as I had nodded at Vera those two months ago. But this time there was nothing wooden or pitying about my nod; it was an awe-filled one of stunning self-discovery. "Ruth," I told the vibrant woman by my side, "*I* am finding that a person is never too old to let go of undesirable, unjustified baggage".

And of course, it was not Ruth I really addressed but myself—because that baggage I was about to let go of had never belonged to Ruth at all, but to me.

"Unless we make Christmas an occasion to share our blessings, all the snow in Alaska won't make it 'white."

– Bing Crosby

"For Christmas this year, try giving less. Start with less attitude. There's more than enough of that in the world as it is – and people will usually just give it back anyway!"

– Anne Bristow

"I get a little behind during Lent, but it comes out even at Christmas."

– Frank Butler

Carol Nordlund Kinsey

Carol is from Breton, a small village in central Alberta, Canada. She currently lives in Winfield, Alberta with her husband, Bryan, two large dogs, and a cat that does not meow.

Over her career, she has written letters to the editor, news and advertising copy, flash fiction, creative non – fiction, romance, wedding scripts, and even a few political speeches. She writes a blog on WordPress that covers whatever topic is timely. She also manages a Facebook page she started the year she was diagnosed with Mastocytosis. The page is dedicated to helping others with similar rare conditions.

Currently, Carol is working as a Marriage Commissioner. She enjoys spending time with her family, a local writer's group 'Wake Up and Write', and as much writing as she can squeeze into her busy life.

Carol can be reached at cnordlundkinsey@gmail.com

Lady in The Tin Foil Hat

By Carol Nordlund Kinsey

"I'll get it!" I yelled when the doorbell rang popping off the couch and rushing for the door. I had been poking and shaking the presents under the tree in anticipation of the grand opening late that evening. Everyone else in the house was off doing other things, my mom and aunt preparing dinner and my uncle working on his Christmas Morning sermon.

Christmas Eve at the minister's house was hectic. My Mom, brother, and I always would arrive late in the afternoon after a full day of shopping and fall into the familiar pattern of wrapping gifts and helping with dinner before the seven o'clock Candlelight Service. This had been the Christmas Eve routine for nine years. My aunt and Uncles house was as familiar to me as my own. We were not guests we were family.

Guests would come and go for days leading up to this night; neighbours and parishioners would drop by to offer season's greetings, sweets, and treats for the local minister and his family. All guests were invited in most would say they were just stopping briefly on their way home or out to a gathering. When the door would close behind them the bustle in the house would pick up again where it left off.

I was sixteen that Christmas, a small-town girl used to small-town ways. My Uncle's church and the manse were a firm reminder of my sheltered life at home.

There was excitement when people came bearing gifts. When the doorbell rang and I jumped to answer it, it never occurred to me that the person on the other side would be anyone but the neighbours or parishioners I expected.

The woman standing under the glow of the porch light, backlit by the frosty streetlights was unlike anyone I had ever seen.

She was dressed in tattered wool. The coat looked like something the Salvation Army would discard as being unsalable. The tiny woman wearing it had lined it with newsprint in an attempt to add extra insulation against the cold. The coat was a feeble excuse for warmth against the bitter night air.

Her hands were covered in mismatched wool gloves, her reddened flesh peeking through a few worn fingertips. She had a holey scarf wound around her neck, the ends tucked into the coat between the layers of newsprint. She had the distinct smell of mothballs and dirt.

As shabbily as she was dressed, her clothes didn't startle me half as much as her Vaseline covered face that gave her a glossy alien appearance and the foil-lined cardboard box that engulfed her head like she was a character in a bad television show.

"Reverend Lemke?" her voice was raspy and thin, her eyes darted like a newly caged animal.

"Um…, Ah…, Uncle Russ? Uncle Russ!" my voice raised an octave with each halted word and brought everyone to the living room. My backward retreat was stalled by the furniture that had been nestled closer together to accommodate the huge tree in front of the picture window.

Much to my relief my beloved uncle magically appeared behind me, my Uncle Russ's tender touch on my shoulders somehow settling the fear and anxiety in my chest.

"Come in," he said to the lady in the tinfoil hat, gently moving me aside to step around me. He guided her in and offered her a seat on the sofa.

She perched on the edge of the cushion, like a cat waiting to be shooed her fingers twisting at invisible threads on her gloves. Her voice barely above a grated whisper as she spoke to my uncle who nodded compassionately, offering gentle words of understanding. He seemed completely unfazed by her appearance.

I had never seen anyone like her and part of me was curious about her circumstance, the other part was frightened by what she was. I stood unabashedly staring at her, my eyes wide and my mouth agape. Everyone around me seemed to behave as if this woman was an everyday visitor to the minister's living room.

The bustle in the house slowed to a crawl, time stood as a sentinel while my uncle ministered to this frail woman. My aunt and mother spoke in hushed tones directing us kids to finish setting the table, making sure we set a place for her. It was quietly understood that our duties were carried out in subdued silence.

She joined us at the table bowing her head in gratitude for the meal. I thought later it was likely her first real meal in days possibly weeks. Her eyes darted around the table looking at each of us. She looked like a scared rabbit encircled by a pack of hungry wolves, fearing that at any minute that she would be attacked and devoured.

When dinner ended and we cleared the table the lady with the tin foil hat disappeared from the house like a skiff of snow on a windshield. The activity accelerated from zero to sixty as we resumed our normal Christmas Eve activities of wrapping gifts and getting ready for the seven o'clock Candlelight Service.

I never saw the lady again. I learned years later at my Uncle's funeral that the lady was a frequent visitor to the manse. She was, as I expected homeless, and was suffering from paranoid schizophrenia. She believed that everyone was out to hurt her, most specifically the government; she also believed that she could find a brief respite from their incessant prying, in the tranquility of my Aunt and Uncle's home.

The lessons from my brief encounter with her were not fully realized until years later, but she is as fresh in my mind today as she was when I opened the door to her glossy Vaseline covered face peering out at me from the inside of her cardboard, foil-lined 'television' hat.

The tenderness and compassion my Uncle showed this frail creature in her time of need was not lost on my adolescent psyche.

The Olympic Turkey

By Carol Nordlund Kinsey

"Darn!!!" was all that came to mind as I stood over the turkey on the floor. That beautiful fifteen-pound turkey I had so lovingly chosen for its full breast and plump legs was splayed under the roaster on the kitchen floor.

This was the first Christmas I was hosting on my own, in my own house. We had moved into our new house only a few months before and this was the first opportunity we had to host a family celebration.

I had spent weeks cleaning, planning, and more cleaning to have the perfect Christmas with my mom and brother.

Our 'new' house was an eighty-year-old station master's house that had been unoccupied for at least five years before we moved in. The only residents prior to us were the four-legged variety. They sounded like they were wearing combat boots as they ran and played in the walls and ceiling. The plumbing banged and sputtered, and the windows didn't close tight but the fire in the woodstove in the basement kept it warm and cozy.

The kitchen was small with the sink on one side and only room enough on the other for an apartment size fridge and stove.

By the time my family arrived on Christmas Eve, the tree was decorated with colored lights and shiny balls. All the gifts I had shopped for were perfectly wrapped and carefully tucked under it. I had spent days ahead of time shopping for our favorite foods, good wine, cheese and crackers, and salsa dip. The turkey was thawing in the fridge and the stuffing was ready.

That evening we sat around the living room listening to Christmas music on the stereo, visiting over a few drinks, and watching Matthew shake the packages trying to guess what was inside. He could open just one present before bed, he made his choice. The box he chose was sparkling red with silver snowflakes. It contained his usual Christmas eve gift, a pair of pajamas and a new book.

Christmas morning, I was up early, the turkey needed to be in the oven if we were going to have dinner on time. I prepared and stuffed it with my favorite stuffing. A recipe passed down to me from my mom. Nestling the turkey into the oversized roaster I borrowed from my husband's grandmother, it barely fit in the small oven.

As my family awoke, we settled around the tree in our housecoats and slippers, spiked coffees in hand to see what surprises were in the brightly colored packages.

With the smell of the turkey beginning to roast mingling with the smell of the bleach I had used to wash the floors and the brewed coffee and baileys in our cups we watched as everyone, in turn, opened a package. The delighted sounds of my family getting things they had asked for echoed through the house and made my heart blossom.

Later after everyone had gotten dressed for the day, the guys were playing a game at the dining room table while my mom helped me peel potatoes, turnip, and carrots for the rest of our dinner. Then it was time to check on the bird.

Oven mitts on, I opened the oven door, pulling the heavy roaster from its sole rack in the oven, and set it on the open oven door. Carefully lifting the lid, I stood up to rest the lid on the stovetop when the turkey, roaster, and all did a full dive off the oven door and landed turkey side down on the floor at my feet.

I was mortified and heartbroken. The special dinner I had spent weeks planning and preparing for was ruined. The half-cooked bird in a messy pile of juices and roaster laid out on the floor. What was I going to do? I had no replacement turkey to cook and a meal of potatoes, turnips, and carrots just would not do.

My mom grabbed a couple of forks, flipped the roaster upright, and popped the turkey back into it. Laughingly she said, 'no one will ever know'. We settled the turkey back into the roaster and pushed it back into the oven.

When dinner was ready, no one else knew the turkey had been rescued from its belly flop on the kitchen floor and it was as delicious.

For years, the disaster of my first Christmas dinner was a secret between my mother and me. Eventually, it became a running joke, whether the turkey had done any Olympic tricks while cooking.

Miriam Roberts

Miriam lives in Drayton Valley, Alberta, Canada, and is a retired Registered Nurse, who met her husband after coming to Canada, has two married sons and two granddaughters.

Along with singing and writing, she likes gardening, family history, volunteering in the community and church. She has traveled to 74 countries before COVID 19 restrictions came into place.

She has also written many articles, for different magazines and newspapers, and wrote a book about her travels. After COVID 19 she joined Wake Up and Write on Zoom from the Drayton Valley Municipal Library.

My Feeling of Christmas

By Miriam Roberts

The anticipation of Christmas starts in the fall when the hoar frost glistens on the trees, in the morning sunshine reflected on the azure blue of the Alberta sky, it looks like a picture-perfect Christmas card.

Once Halloween is over Christmas decorations start appearing in the stores, on people's houses and streets decked with garlands as on cue to the song of my native Wales, Deck the Halls with Boughs of Holly is being piped into the air. Christmas items start appearing in the stores giving the feeling of Christmas, although this is giving way to online shopping.

Depending on the tradition you follow, you may be practicing Christmas songs emphasizing the birth of the Christ Child in preparation of the day of his birth.

The pagan celebration of the winter holiday called Yule, moved from the winter solstice and became aligned with the Christmas celebration, together adding a possible influence of the ancient Roman tradition of honoring the god Saturn when gifts were exchanged adding this dimension to the present-day Christmas celebration.

The Christmas tradition of having an evergreen tree has been adopted by people of Canada, regardless of their origins, and appears in late November until at least twelve days after Christmas. The tree has pagan origins with the use of the branches being used at the winter solstice and for Christians, the evergreen tree represents the everlasting life of God.

Christmas trees traditionally were decorated with candles representing stars, candies, coloured paper, apples, and candy canes to name a few. The candles were replaced with electric lights for safety reasons. Stars represent the star of Bethlehem guiding the wise men to the birthplace of Jesus, angels could be placed atop to announce Jesus birth on the first Christmas. Candy canes, the white represents the purity of Jesus Christ and the red the blood, when he died on the cross. Families may make their own decorations and keep them until no longer useful or attractive. I developed my own tradition of buying Christmas tree decorations from different countries I visited.

Holly boughs represent the crown of thorns that Jesus wore when he was crucified and the berries represent the drops of blood that were shed by Jesus because of the thorns. Ivy may also be added to decorating the home as the female counterpart. Mistletoe in the Western world is associated with Christmas as a decoration. The custom of kissing under the mistletoe started in Victorian England.

Sending and receiving greetings is central to the feeling of goodwill in this season, the colourfull cards are sent and received from all over the world, hearing from friends and relatives not heard from the rest of the year is a treat. It's an opportunity to catch up on what has happened during the year, whether by card, letter, email, phone call, or even social media.

Baking is a tradition I have kept, although making plum pudding, Christmas cake and mince pies have been replaced by making shortbread cookies, chocolate chip with added cocoa cookies, butter tarts, and pies. Some of these are sold at our church Christmas bake sale while others are given to shut-ins and while some are saved to serve to family and company during this festive season. A pie I have been making is bumbleberry, which has been become a favourite for our family at any time of the year and at sales. This pie has apple, rhubarb, raspberry, strawberry, and blueberry which can be replaced by any other berry of choice. Instead of pie crust on top, I have used crumble topping spiced with ground cloves and cinnamon, served with ice cream.

Coming back to singing, after a fall of practicing the choir I sing in gives a concert early in December to the public in a theatre and also goes to the seniors' residences, it is pleasing to see their faces light up during the performances. Singing is a part of the tradition I keep, and sing at the seniors' long-term care facility once a week until Christmas, giving them a rendition of the carols and Christmas songs, they have known is a part of keeping Christmas alive for me. At one time I would go singing carols around the houses and we would have mince tarts to follow.

I have already mentioned the giving of gifts, which is now most important to a child's Christmas, gifts were given to the Christ child by the Wise men. In Southern Europe Saint Nicholas of the 3rd century secretly gave gifts, his model could have given rise to Santa Claus of the present day. Children are encouraged to visit Santa Claus from a young age in the malls or at parties, they tell him what they would like to have for Christmas. Christmas eve is when he magically travels on a sleigh from the North Pole through the air, pulled by up to eight reindeer, and squeezes down the chimney to leave the presents under the Christmas tree. Children leave some milk and cookies for Santa and are happy to see he ate the cookies and milk and leaving behind the gifts they wished for. The opening of the gifts is such an exciting time, with wrapping paper being strewn in all directions.

Adults give gifts as well and gift exchanges occur, while some adults will forego giving of actual gifts in exchange for giving monetary gifts to charities of their choice. Now that my own children are adults who have all they need, I buy them a small gift and give a donation to a charity with the rest of the money I would spend on them. As my grandchildren grew up, I would give them a small gift and give them some money to buy what they need.

The expectation of giving at Christmas is generally a custom that can be carried to the extreme resulting in heavy debt in the New Year. One does not need to be a miser like the legendary Ebenezer Scrooge of Charles' Dickens novella, A Christmas Carol who disliked family gatherings, seasonal food and drink, and a festive generosity of spirit. I have known people to have a wonderful Christmas with homemade gifts and without the extravagance of excesses of food and beverages.

Christmas would not be complete without going to church either on Christmas eve or Christmas day to celebrate the birth of the Christ Child. Singing well-known carols add to the celebration, completing the Christmas feeling.

Feasting is a big part of the tradition of Christmas. As a child, we would have a goose for dinner, but it was replaced with a turkey and all the trimmings. Hundreds of years ago a decorated boar's head would be served upon a platter, tusks, and all. The next day I love eating the cold turkey with cranberry sauce and salads, it comes with so little preparation after cooking the big festive meal. A turkey pot pie made with the scraps, and boiling up the bones says goodbye to Christmas.

During the week between Christmas and New year as a family, board and card games are often played as well as putting together a jigsaw puzzle.

When January comes, I say I am not going to spend as much time and money on the next Christmas as I pack up all the decorations and clean up. When fall rolls around again the feeling of the celebration of a new birth makes me forget the laborious preparations for Christmas like one forgets the pain of giving birth to your own child!

"My idea of Christmas, whether old-fashioned or modern, is very simple: loving others. Come to think of it, why do we have to wait for Christmas to do that?"

– Bob Hope

"I bought my brother some gift wrap for Christmas. I took it to the gift wrap department and told them to wrap it, but in a different print so he would know when to stop unwrapping."

– Steven Wright

"Sending Christmas cards is a good way to let your friends and family know that you think they're worth the price of a stamp."

– Melanie White

Lillian Ross

Lillian Ross is a writer of historical novels, all of which are based in Alberta and are true accounts of adventures in the Northwest. The stories, creative mixes of fact and fiction, are the result of many years of collecting and researching, using written memoirs, history books, letters, archival documents, and interviews.

Lillian attended the University of Alberta and attained a Bachelor of Education. She taught for many years before retiring to pursue her writing. She married Reg Ross and they had two sons, Lonnie and Erin, who live and work in Alberta. As well as writing, teaching, community service and raising a family, she enjoys music and has sung and played in a band with her husband for many years as well as a musical band of women.

Lillian has completed the sequel to Gandy Dancer, based on her and her husband's life in the oilfield. It is called
I Kept Falling in the Sink and is a memoir of their lives.

Christmas In The Great Depression
By Lillian Ross

At Christmas time in 1930, Sadie and Donald had tried hard to give their children special treats to eat as well as something in their stockings, even if it meant going without something else. They had thirteen children, six of them at the age where they believed Santa still filled their socks. Going to bed earlier every night so that the lamp didn't have to be lit, was one way to conserve on coal oil. Doing without shoes, and wearing patched rubber boots stuffed with wool, or going to bed early so that Mumma could wash their overalls and sew them up, so they could put them on to wear to school the next day, were other ways.

But Sadie could not conserve on coal oil because often it was after the children went to bed that she found time to stitch up something that could be a gift for their Christmas stockings, as well as being something that they needed to keep them warm. Spinning and knitting late at night could produce a woolly doll, mitts, socks, or toques. Seven-year-old Lawrence had waited, standing on one foot, for his mumma to finish knitting the other sock before he could go to school.

In 1930, people were still generous to the extent that they supplied enough for a small gift for each child for Christmas. The School Board had a full Santa's sack of brown paper bags with an orange, an apple, and candies. On top of that, some got whistles and balls; others got combs and hair ribbons, colouring books and crayons, mirrors, and various small toys.

After the concert, for which they had practiced every afternoon the whole month of December, Santa, burst through the door with a hearty 'Ho ho ho!' and his heavy sack of goodies. Six-year-old Reta's eyes glowed when she saw him. He came – he really came! In their school concert play, where they had built the chimney for Santa out of cardboard boxes, and Lenny Allen, playing the role of Santa in the play, had come crashing through the boxes, she had thought it would all be 'pretend' – he wouldn't really come to their school! But here he was!

When he handed Reta a bag of candies with an apple and an orange, she was ecstatic. But as he handed her a present gaily wrapped in red paper and string, she could not believe her eyes; it had her name on it – there was no mistake. Santa boomed out, "I'll bet you thought I'd never get here. Well, I had a hard time rounding up those reindeer of mine. They all thought they were going to fly south for the winter. Why Donder and Blitzen hid in the barn! They said, 'Surely he won't take us out on a night like this!' But I said, 'Come on Dancer and Prancer, shake the cobwebs outa yer heads. Those kids at Meadowview School have been good all year long, and they're gonna get some gifts this year if I have to hitch a ride on a Canada goose!'"

Everyone laughed. Jack Payne was always a funny Santa. Everyone loved him. While the children were gathered around Santa and opening their gifts, the women were setting out lunch. They had all brought something, and it ended up being a veritable feast: chicken, home-cured ham, bread, butter and cakes, jars of pickles, jam, and jelly. They couldn't sell it, someone had commented dryly, but they could enjoy eating it. And this was a special time – a time for putting on the special things saved for special circumstances.

Reta opened her parcel carefully, trying not to tear the pretty paper or break the red string. She was going to save it all and take it home. When she got the parcel open, her heart skipped a beat. She must be dreaming! There on the red paper lay a little doll with a perfect little china head, and a stuffed cloth body. The hair was of the same material as the face, painted and shaped so that it almost looked real. But the face! It was so beautiful! Tiny little pink cheeks and a rosy, pouty mouth, a tiny perfect nose, and wide blue eyes made this the most beautiful doll she had ever seen. And Santa Claus had given it to *her!*

She hugged it to her chest while her sisters, Gladys and Dona, crowded around to see what she had gotten. They showed her their gifts: an embroidered hanky, a mirror, a little shell necklace, and a huge red hair ribbon, but she was sure that nothing could compare to her doll.

Reta's eyes were wet as she showed her Mumma, but she wouldn't give the doll up, even for a second so that someone else could see. "I've got some scraps of cloth left from Mary's dress," her Mumma told her. "I'll make your baby some doll clothes." Reta's eyes shone with delight, and she couldn't wait to get home to play with her. Katie and Murdy also received gifts from Santa even though they were not old enough to be in school. Katie had received a little doll, but it was not like Reta's. It was a rag doll with a painted face, button eyes, and a mop cap sewed on to the top of the head.

The School Board had gone 'all out' this year. As The Great Depression deepened, however, the budget would get slimmer and slimmer until they were afraid that Santa's gifts would be a thing of the past.

After Christmas, temperatures plummeted and it took all the stoves, filled to capacity, going full time to keep the house and the boys' shack warm. Everyone cuddled into their beds as long as they could to stay warm in the mornings until the heater was glowing before they reluctantly eased themselves out of the warm covers and hurried to surround the stove, where they shivered into their cold clothes. After hot porridge and bundling up in their warm sweaters and socks, they reluctantly faced the cold and hurried the quarter of a mile to school, thankful all the while that they didn't live as far away as most of the other children.

Sometimes, when it was extremely cold, the MacIntoshes, the Allens, who lived right across the road, and the teacher, who roomed with the Allens, were the only ones in school. They spent all day crowding around the red-hot, pot-bellied stove with their feet up off the floor, and their desks dragged up so close that their faces were red, but their backs were cold. The cold seeped in and crept across the floor and up the walls. When they hurried home after school, they crowded around the heater again and only left it to go out to do the chores. They even ate around the heater.

Water for the animals was a challenge. The river, sloughs, and ponds were frozen over, so it meant hauling up water from the well and hauling it to the barn by the bucketful. Richard, Willie, and Ewen, when they got home, were kept busy hauling water, hay and straw to the animals. When they weren't doing that, they were sawing and chopping up more wood to feed the hungry stoves, or they were hauling in snow to melt on top of the stove for household use. The snow was melted to wash clothes, dishes, floors and to bathe in, as they crowded around the heater, while someone held up a blanket for another to bathe behind. You were required to conserve everything. If a tubful of soapy water was not too dirty after a washing or a rinsing, it was used to bathe in or wash the floor.

Loath to leave the heater at night, they undressed by it, toasted themselves thoroughly, and then ran to jump into their cold bed. Mary still slept on the couch with Murdy, while Dona, Reta, and Katie crawled in at the head of the bed, and Lawrence, Ewen, and Gladys slept at the foot. They warmed their feet against the feet of the person above or below them.

When the older ones got up first in the morning to go about their chores, Reta and Katie would cuddle up a while longer, unwilling to face the cold until they had to. Then Murdy, left alone after Mary got up, would creep in beside them. Unwilling to put their feet on the floor, but too wide-awake to get up, they would curl up, talk and giggle.

"What did you dream latht night?" Reta lisped one morning as she wrapped her dolly, that she called Annie, in the little blanket, and placed her between them next to her face. They would often tell each other their dreams when they dallied in bed in the mornings. If they couldn't remember their dreams, they would make one up.

"I dreamed," Katie dragged out the words as though she couldn't quite remember, "that I was walking up these long stairs in this great big house, and Mumma was at the top of the stairs. She said, 'This is our new house.' She told me that one room was mine, one was yours and one was the boys' room. In my room, there was a tall cupboard with toys and clothes all the way to the top. And she handed me down a doll. It looked just like your Annie, but mine had long golden hair, eyes that opened and shut and it could really cry."

"Ith that a true dream or did you make that up?" Reta demanded. Though she tried, she could not get over her lisp, likely because of her two front teeth.

Then Katie dissolved into giggles, and she wriggled all over, winding the blankets around her. "I just made that up. You didn't say whether it was supposed to be a real dream or a made-up one." Then she giggled again and Reta joined her.

"I dreamed," Reta started off with a spooky, hushed voice, "that I wath running down thith dark path through the buth when I thaw a big thadow up ahead. I knew it wath a bear! I turned around and thtarted running for home, but I couldn't get my legth to run fatht. They would only move thlowly, and it wath like trying to pull them out of the mud. I could hear the bear coming clother, and I tried harder to get my legth to work, but they wouldn't move. I tried to thcream but all I could do wath thqueak. Then jutht ath the bear wath going to pounthe on me – I woke up!" Reta finished with a pause and a flourish of her hands.

"Don't have dreams like that, okay?" Katie told her seriously, "They're too scary." And she shivered.

"Okay," Reta agreed. Then they both dissolved into another spasm of giggles.

"Telling dreams again?" Lawrence wanted to know, as he popped his head over the edge of the bed, coming up with his sock that had found its way underneath.

"You didn't have any more dreams about big white horses, did you?" he asked with devilish glee.

"No," Katie pouted. "Go do your chores!" The moment was spoiled for Katie. She'd made the mistake of telling Lawrence that she'd dreamed about riding a big white horse and then getting off to go into the bush to squat. When she woke up, she discovered that she'd wet the bed.

Mumma was so mad at her! "You're getting to be too big a girl to wet the bed anymore. Now, look at what you've done! We're going to have to wash the sheets and turn the mattress over. It's too cold to take it outside to wash it now. If you had got up earlier to the 'pail', that wouldn't have happened. You drank too much water last night."

Katie was so embarrassed. She didn't know that would happen if you dreamed about a white horse. And Lawrence had nodded his head seriously, all-knowing in his advanced age of seven, and said, "That's one of the worst things you can do is go back to sleep when something wakes you, and you dream that you're getting up."

She couldn't remember dreaming of getting up. She did remember Murdy crying in the night and getting a spanking because he wouldn't stay in his own bed but kept crawling into Mumma and Puppa's bed. 'But,' Katie thought, 'I went right back to sleep, and that wasn't when I had the dream. That was last year when Murdy was not even three. He's nearly four now.'

The fun was spoiled. "I guess I have to get up anyway." And she slid out to find the chamber pail under the bed.

After they dressed around the heater, had their breakfasts, and washed the dishes, Katie and Reta returned to the heater. On the shelf above the trunk was the spot where Reta kept her china doll so that it would be safe while she was at school. She took it carefully out of the blankets in the bed, climbed on top of the trunk, and tucked the doll as high as she could reach onto the shelf. There sat Annie with her head slumped over onto her chest, and her legs dangling over the edge of the shelf. "Mumma, don't let Katie or Murdy play with my doll while I'm at school," she always reminded her Mumma. "They might break her."

Katie wouldn't touch her sister's doll anyway – she knew how Reta felt about that. But just in case her Mumma might see the doll and hand it down to either of the little ones, Reta felt everyone needed a reminder. Murdy, she didn't trust, and Katie just might have an accident.

Above her, Mumma and Pappu's dresser was another wide shelf where a lot of the clean clothes were kept. More warm stockings were put up there, and she needed another pair to go on over top of the ones she had. She'd been cold yesterday going to school with just one pair. Katie wouldn't be going out today - maybe she'd wear hers. She grabbed a chair and carried it over to the dresser with her. Just as she got to the curtained entrance to Mumma's bedroom area, she had a sudden thought. Lawrence had just come in out of the cold after bringing in an armload of wood to the wood box and a tubful of snow. He'd come over to the heater and was warming his hands as Reta removed the chair that was right behind him.

'Did Lawrence plan to sit down on that chair?' Reta wondered, and she turned back just in time to hear a thump, and see her brother land hard on the board floor. He'd decided to take off his socks and warm up his toes to the fire, but the chair that he'd stood in front of seconds before was suddenly gone. The jar caused him to bite his tongue and nearly knocked the wind out of him. Not to mention the landing that jolted and injured every bone in his body. So shocked was he, that he lay there for a few seconds assessing the damage.

He turned his head to see his sister standing six feet away with the chair in her hands, and she had the nerve to smile! Now he was angry. That was malicious! He could have been badly hurt. "What did you do that for!" he shouted, as he scrambled to his feet. "I was going to sit on that! You knew I was going to sit there. You did that on purpose. That hurt!"

"No, I didn't," Reta started to defend herself, but she couldn't keep the grin from tugging at the corners of her mouth. He looked so funny! She tried not to smile because she knew that he had fallen hard and that he was very angry with her, but she couldn't help it.

"Gimme that!" he bellowed, as he snatched the chair from her, making her stagger back, and he limped back to the heater, rubbing his legs and backside and making pained noises. When he glanced back and saw that she was trying not to grin, he stepped up his tirade. Red in the face, he advanced a step or two saying, "Look out, if I get a chance to play a trick like that on you, Reta! Just you look out!"

Reta wiped the smile off her face, retreating to the safety of the kitchen and her Mumma's skirts. 'I think I'll steer clear of Lawrence for a while,' she thought. 'But,' she grinned that wicked little buck-toothed grin again to herself; 'he looked so funny!' The trickster had been tricked.

Reta woke up one morning feeling very sick. The bed was trying to turn around in circles, and her stomach was in danger of turning over. "Don't thake the bed," she'd whispered to Katie. "Be thtill."

But the sun was shining outside and the water was running in the ditches. Katie was anxious to go outside after breakfast with Murdy and play since it was so nice. She couldn't convince her sister so she bounded out of bed, and scooted in behind the long kitchen table to eat her porridge.

"Why isn't Reta here at breakfast?" Mumma asked. "It's just about time to leave for school."

"She doesn't feel good" Katie answered, popping another spoonful into her mouth and glancing out the window as she saw the O'Neills going by on the road.

Sadie went immediately to the bed and touched her daughter's shoulder. When Reta turned feverish eyes to her, Sadie felt her forehead. "Katie says you're sick."

Reta nodded, then looked agitated. "I'm gonna throw up." Her Mumma barely got back in time with the basin before Reta vomited. While her Mumma held her forehead, Reta leaned her head over the edge of the bed until her stomach stopped its rebellion.

Her Mumma wiped her face with a warm washcloth, straightened the tangled sheets and blankets around her, and closed the door behind Katie and Murdy as they ran out to play. Reta felt so much better. She was comfortable, her stomach had settled down, and the house was so quiet she could hear the fire sputtering softly in the heater and the clock ticking. Her Mumma sat down to her spinning wheel and Reta listened to the click and whirr of the spindle and the treadle under her foot.

Closing her eyes, Reta tried to find sleep in the gentle hum of the quiet house. How many times had she gotten up early on a cold winter morning and wished that she could just roll back into that warm bed, let everybody else go to school without her, and just lie there listening to the quiet as she went back to sleep? Now, her eyes wouldn't stay shut. They popped back open and she stared at the logs, the shelf on the wall, and then the rafters in the ceiling. Watching a fly buzzing around the room, she heard the bark of a dog in the distance. It was so hard just to lie there!

She felt so much better! Why didn't she just jump up, say, 'Mumma I'm all better now,' get dressed, and eat her breakfast? She was starting to feel like she could eat some porridge. But she couldn't do that. Her Mumma would say that she might as well get to school then – it wasn't too late. And Lawrence would say that she was just trying to stay home from school so she could play. 'I'm prob'ly still sick anyway,' she told herself, and she rolled over again to face the wall.

She couldn't keep her eyes shut; were only looking at the inside of her eyelids. But she just couldn't *lie* here any longer. Listening to Katie and Murdy shouting and playing out by the stream beside the muskeg, she decided that she was tired of lying in her bed. She tossed around, but then her Mumma glanced over at her so she forced herself to lie still, and stare at the wall again.

Finally, she sat up. "Are you feeling better?" her Mumma asked from the spinning wheel as she drew the strands of wool out, and spun them into a thin braided strand.

"Yeth, I'm lotth better now," her daughter admitted.

"Would you like some breakfast?"

"Yeth, I think I'm hungry."

"All right. You get up and get dressed and I'll dish you up some porridge. Here's some nice warm water to wash in and I'll comb your hair."

After breakfast, Reta looked up at the clock. It was ten o'clock. It was too late to be sent to school now. "Can I go outthide with Murdy and Katie now?"

"All right, but don't get yourself cold and wet or you'll end up back in bed."

Reta was dressed warm and out the door in a flash and running around to the back of the house, where Katie and Murdy were building a snow-fort. It seemed no time at all until it was noon and her sisters and brothers were home from school, bubbling with all the funny things that had happened, and all the things that people had said.

No one paid much attention to Reta. It was as though they'd forgotten that she hadn't attended school. Finally, in a lull in the conversation, Gladys said to Reta, "Miss Miller asked where you were and Mary said you were sick." Five pairs of eyes turned on Reta and she shrunk.

"I'm feeling better now," she said softly, as she stared at the food on her plate and pushed it around.

Reta breathed again when they were out the door and running back to school. Not even Lawrence had teased her about playing hooky. The three little ones bubbled with plans to play in the straw that Richard had hauled in from Crotteau's.

Reta had not given another thought to her absenteeism until they were running across the barnyard toward the house and they heard talking. She looked out toward the road, and there were Edith and Donald O'Neill, Cora MacLean, and Doris Barnhouse. They were looking at her, but they were not smiling. She paused in the middle of her race, fairly skidding to a stop, and stared back at the children in horror. She'd been caught! They knew! She wasn't sick. They'd tell Miss Miller that Mary had lied to her. She was so embarrassed and ashamed of herself. Hanging her head, she turned away and walked to the house.

 Lawrence, for a while after his tumble, used to tease Reta that he was going to take her doll down off the shelf and run away with it. Reta worried about that, but she didn't have another safe place to keep it without putting it in danger, so she climbed up onto the trunk every morning after he was out of the way and off to school, and tucked Annie back up on the shelf. She made sure she got home before Lawrence and took her down to pack the doll along with her so she would be safe. She need not have been quite so diligent, because Lawrence soon forgot about the incident and the doll. He had other things to occupy his attention.

One day when Reta ran home from school and climbed up to get her precious black-haired doll, she slipped just as she reached for her. Someone had come in the door right behind her and startled her. She struggled to keep herself from falling off the rounded trunk surface and scrambled to keep Annie from falling out of her hands. She was successful at neither. Down she crashed to the floor and down fell the china doll crashing to the hard surface of the trunk. She had bruised her shin and skinned her arm, but she'd hardly felt that. Picking up the shattered shards of the china doll's face she blinked back huge tears that filled her eyes. Her beautiful Annie had but a floppy grey-cloth body and no head. The perfect little face with the rosy cheeks and mouth were shattered beyond repair. The blue eyes were ghastly blue marbles that rolled across the floor.

The person who had come in behind her was Lawrence. He looked down into the crushed countenance of his little sister as she held the pink shards in hands that were bleeding with cuts, and he felt like crying himself. As angry as he had been with his sister, he never in his life would have wanted something like this to happen to her. They gazed at each other for a minute with a shared compassion before Reta dissolved in tears at his feet.

Then his Mumma was there, and Mary and Katie to help pick up the shattered pieces of Reta and her doll. Turning and running to the barn, Lawrence climbed to the loft, threw himself down onto the hay, and as the kittens climbed all over him, he stroked them and said over and over, "I'm sorry. I'm sorry!"

Lillian Ross October 2 - 1931 to November 16 - 2020.

Singer, Songwriter, Retired Music Teacher, Published Author, Beloved Community Member

Lillian, or Lily to her close friends, wrote historical fiction and is locally well-known and loved for her sunny disposition, a long list of self-published books, articles in magazines, and a love for her fellow human being.

Lily could turn a writing assignment into a song and a favorite example of this is when the writers were asked to create a piece using the following prompt: Harry Potter meets Jesus in a Starbucks line-what did they talk about?

She brought her guitar to our next program and we sang the hymn she created!

Everyone loved it!

Lilly was often leading Wake Up & Write! and The Write Stuff members in song, playing with her band at local venues or, doing any number of good works like reading to friends at the local senior's lodge, volunteering as Secretary for the 55+ Club or, finding entertainment for the Oil Wives.

I once had the honor to share the stage with Lily in a production of the Vagina Monologues.

I know she is proud of the members of Wake Up & Write! The Write Stuff having our work in Make A Joyful Noise and would wish to thank Sue for the opportunity-Thank you, Sue!

By Leah Sanderson
Lily's friend and Facilitator of Wake Up & Write! The Write Stuff, A Drayton Valley Libraries program since 2011.

"Our hearts grow tender with childhood memories and love of kindred, and we are better throughout the year for having, in spirit, become a child again at Christmastime."

--Laura Ingalls Wilder

"I hate the radio this time of year because they play "All I Want For Christmas Is You" like, every other song. And that's just not enough."

– Bridger Winegar

"Christmas is a magical time of year... I just watched all my money magically disappear."

– Unknown

Karen Probert

Karen Probert's first two published books - "Fragments of Lives" (2011) and "Colouring our Lives" (2014) - are filled with short stories about people who's dreams and lives may seem ordinary on the surface but, as in real life, there are undercurrents that cause these characters to rethink their lives or actions. Her third published book, "Bloodlines" (2018) goes deeper into the life of an anthropologist as she delves into a foreign culture while trying to also find the roots of her own family.

Karen writes wherever she is at the time – often home in Sherwood Park or Canmore, Alberta, Canada, or on trips to other places. Her books are available from dreamwritepublishing.ca. Karen is a founding member and currently Past President of the Writers Foundation of Strathcona County (WFSC), Alberta (wfscsherwoodpark.com). She and two other members have co-written a workbook "Your Lifetime of Stories, Ideas for Writing Memoirs" which is available through WFSC.

A Memorable Day

By Karen Probert

When the phone rang at seven Christmas morning Evelyn knew something was wrong. She was certainly right.

"Mom, hope I didn't wake you. I started putting things in the car and saw that it had a flat tire. Had to take everything out to change it, etcetera, etcetera. Long story short we're just leaving. The roads look good. We'll be there at about nine. Okay?"

"Of course, dear. Drive carefully, Karl. There'll be fresh coffee when you get here. It's going to be a memorable day"

Ev decided to make a pot of coffee now and a fresh one later. As she passed the front door on her way downstairs she flicked on the outside lights. She had set the coffeemaker the night before so now just clicked it 'ON'.

"It's going to be a memorable day," she sang to herself as she went into the bathroom to brush her teeth.

Coming back into the kitchen she instantly saw coffee puddling across the white marble counter, draining down between the cabinet and the stove where it pooled on the creamy tiles. "Damn that loose basket," she muttered as she turned the machine off and threw dishtowels onto the hot, brown mess.

As she watched a new pot brewing, Ev cleaned the counter, cupboard front, and floor. Ignoring the stain soaking into the hem of her robe where it had met the coffee puddle on the floor, she made an effort to just stand still to let the joy of

Christmas fill her mind. Instead, she heard Charlie's uneven footfalls and then the shower running.

With a cup of fresh coffee in her hand, and having tucked the wet corner of her robe into her pocket, Ev entered the living room. In the pale glow of the nightlight, she'd left on Ev saw the grey mouse skitter out from under the tree, race across the hearth, and disappear into the fireplace. *'We'll roast that little beast when we fire it up later'* ran through her mind.

When her thumb pushed the switch to turn on the tree lights a crackling sound preceded almost imperceptibly the shock to her hand. As she pulled back some of her coffee sloshed onto a large, rectangular, shiny red parcel. "Damn. Charles will have to reset the breaker again. Maybe I did put too many lights on the tree-like he said."

Using the other corner of her already damp robe, Ev mopped up the bit of coffee, repositioned the large bow on the parcel, and set it back under the tree. That's when she saw the small clumps of scattered green and gold foil paper. Digging behind some parcels and gathering up the bits she saw that the mouse had chewed a hole in a package of chocolates destined for her mother-in-law. Ev scooped up the parcel, headed into the den where she'd done all her wrapping. Using a small basket and some snowflake patterned cellophane Evelyn piled the uneaten Ferrero Roche chocolates into a pyramid-shaped pile and tied a green ribbon on top with the tag. The mouse had only nibbled into two of the rich delicacies and Ev was sure that Ruth wouldn't count them.

From the kitchen came a crash followed by Charlie's groan and then, "Oh, hell, Ev. Help!" She raced there to find Charles hanging onto the counter with one hand, his other hand clutching the fridge door handle. His slippered left foot was splayed out in front of him while the cast on his right ankle curled behind where it had slipped on the freshly mopped tile. Putting her hands under his armpits she lifted while he resettled his feet under his considerable girth.

"Good morning, my sweet. Thank you. I see we've had another coffee disaster. Good thing I put a new coffeemaker under the tree. Oops! I wasn't supposed to tell you that was I?"
"That's a great gift, Charles. I'll be pleased. Don't worry. I know how to feign surprise. Before you have coffee could you reset the breaker for the tree, please? It gave me a shock already when it tripped." *'Or maybe that mouse chewed on the cord'.*

While Charles clumped towards the electrical panel in the back hall, Ev scooted upstairs and into the shower. It had to be a short one as Charles had used up most of the hot water. Ev thought for the millionth time that maybe it was time to move to a newer, smaller place where all the equipment was modern and there would be no stairs for Charles to slip and break his foot. *'But we love this house. We have so many wonderful memories here. So there'll be no thoughts about moving today. Today we'll just make more memories to share. It's going to be a memorable day.'*

Evelyn had planned to wear the red silk overshirt Karl's wife Kate had given her last year but at an early Christmas party someone had spilled red wine on the sleeve and Ev had forgotten to pick it up at the cleaners. She wouldn't worry about it. Instead, she'd wear the red sweater with a snowflake pattern that Kate had given her the year before. Red made Evelyn look pale and drawn but Kate always gave her something red for Christmas despite the hints during the year. As Evelyn drew the sweater over her head it caught on her earring and she couldn't get it untangled. Carrying her glasses while holding the sweater away from one eye Ev slowly descended to the kitchen to ask Charles to disengage her. His booming laugh while his bulky fingers managed the delicate procedure made Ev giggle.

Wearing a special Christmas apron, she checked that the tree was lit up before she put bacon on to cook in the electric frying pan. Charles was in the family room filling the stockings, his favourite Christmas job, before hanging them along the mantle. She'd take a photo before they were opened. A piece of bacon splattered grease on the back of her hand. As she ran it under cold water she thought *'It's going to be a memorable day with Karl and Kate and my perfect grandbabies and my cherished Charles. We'll have so much fun'.*

Some of the bacon was a bit overly crisp as she settled it in the oven while she prepared eggs for French toast – a Christmas morning tradition since Karl was a little boy. She looked at the clock and called out to Charles "Where are they? It's ten past nine already. They should be here. I'm fretting."

Taking her camera into the family room Evelyn snapped a photo just as Charles hung the last of the seven stockings. They felt a rush of cold air so Evelyn turned towards the front door to snap a photo just as Karl, Kate, and kids burst through it calling "Merry Christmas. We're here. Did Santa come to your house? Oh, it's going to be a memorable day!"

Christmas Eve

By Karen Probert

Jennifer lay quietly, breathing deeply so it would seem that she was sleeping. Just in case anyone checked or was listening, or even cared. Her left foot itched so she rubbed it against the warm sheet where the raised edge of the mattress pushed up. That didn't really relieve the itching but it felt good to be doing something, anything but just lying here.

She had at least another hour before she would be able to get up, open the door, creep along the wall of the upstairs hall to get to the top of the stairs. One day last week she had practised doing that. The floor was almost silent right along the side where it met the wall. Not like in the middle where the floor creaked and snapped when you ran across it. The stairs were exactly seventeen steps from her bedroom door. The stairs had been a practising place too. Jennifer had walked up and down the middle, down the left side, up and down the right side, even from one side of each step to the other to find places where she could step without making the stairs crackle and groan as she moved over them. The idea to sit down and slide on her pajama covered bottom from one step to the next was a revelation when she realized that it was almost soundless.

Jennifer could hear quiet voices from the living room. Her mother and Arnie were talking and sometimes laughing a bit. She knew when Arnie needed another beer as the couch cushion made a swooshy noise as he got up, then she heard his heavy feet crossing the hall, then the fridge door creaking open against the broken hinge before the bottles clinked together and the door was closed with a groan and a clank. By straining she could even hear the expulsion of air and bubbles from the bottle after the opener popped the top off. This house muffled no sounds.

That is what made these sounds comfortable – they were everyday sounds now, calm sounds, gentle sounds. Not like last Christmas Eve. That was the last time she'd seen her father. He had spent that afternoon musing with a bottle of ten-year-old scotch he'd been given by a customer. When her mother had arrived home he had tried to stand up but it took four attempts for him to get out of his chair. By then his face was angry and red. Jennifer's mother had protested when he tried to kiss her and put his hand on her bottom. Jennifer's mother had said, "Not here, for heaven's sake, the child is watching and you're drunk as a skunk." Her voice was calm but there was a bitterness underneath which Jennifer didn't understand.

Her mother had asked "You got the present today, right?" and then she looked at Jennifer's father and said resignedly, "Rob, the stores are closed now. You promised. You promised that you'd do it, that you would at least do that. You didn't. Now it's too late. It's too late for anything! Rob, listen to me. Go to your mother's or somewhere now. And don't come back. Just don't ever come back."

Jennifer had heard her father yell, heard her mother cry, heard her father wail and break things, heard her mother call 911, then heard the sirens and policemen. She stayed under her bed until her mother came to find her. Her mother was shaking and the bloody line on her face was raw looking. Her mother just held Jennifer on the bed until they both fell asleep.

The next morning was Christmas. Jennifer's stocking was full of candies, an orange, Jumping Jacks, a red, white, and blue India rubber ball, a new skipping rope with bright pink handles, and some hair ribbons. Under the tree was a beautiful brown ringletted doll with real glass eyes from her Grandmother Pearce in England. There was a new pale yellow dress that she had heard her mother sewing for her nights after she'd gone to bed. Jennifer had even seen some tiny scraps of yellow fabric and so hoped it would be the pattern with the puffed sleeves. It was. There was a present from England for her mother too – a soft wool paisley shawl in mauve and beige. In another parcel were three books and some crayons from her father's mother, Grandy, who worked at the library and got to take home books that were in nearly new condition but that no one wanted to borrow. There was no box from Santa Claus, no red wrapping paper and silver ribbon to savour before opening it, no BIG gift as Jennifer's mother said on the telephone with Auntie Sue later that day.

Jennifer knew that BIG gifts didn't really come from Santa Claus. BIG gifts were the treasures that your mother wanted you to have especially but that were costly so you had to wait until the last paycheque of the year to pick them up from layaway. Daddy was supposed to pick up the pale blue bike last year but he didn't. Jennifer's mother picked it up in January so Jennifer had been able to ride it all summer after she learned to keep her balance. It was a wonderful bike and she loved it but knew that her mother was very disappointed that Christmas day had been ruined by not having it there.

This year Jennifer thought that Arnie wouldn't forget to pick up a present. She had heard her mother remind him in the morning and he had promised! Jennifer just wanted to creep down the stairs to see it was there in its red paper with a silver ribbon. She didn't want her mother to look like last year, with makeup not really covering her bruised cheek and black eye. She didn't want to see her mother's flat sad eyes and slightly shaky hands while she told her sister she would divorce Rob. Jennifer's mother and Auntie Sue cried a lot last Christmas.

Arnie had brought light back into Jennifer's mother's eyes and a smile to her lips. His laughter helped Jennifer feel safe again. He wouldn't forget the present, she just knew he wouldn't forget the present. Christmas could be Christmas again if he just didn't forget the present.

Raymond Anthony Fernando

Raymond Anthony Fernando is a motivational speaker, poet, author, trainer, songwriter, freelance television actor, ghostwriter, media celebrity and a regular newspaper forum page writer. He is a Mental Health Ambassador with the Institute of Mental Health; and is Singapore's leading advocate for the mentally ill. The author of 40 books was married to Doris Lau authored 8 books. Raymond who was chosen as Model Caregiver 2007 and Mental Health Champion 2010 is born on Valentine's Day and is a contributing writer to the Buddhist Temple's magazine, AWAKEN. He has contributed 31 years service in the public sector, has 15 years experience in public relations work and has received several awards and commendations from government organisations. Raymond attributes his success to two wonderful people – his beloved wife, Doris and his dear mother Mrs. Pearl Donna Fernando – both of whom have made a huge impact on his life.

The most wonderful time of the year

By Raymond Anthony Fernando

"Christmas is not in tinsel and lights and outward show. The secret lies in an inner glow. It's lighting a fire inside the heart. Goodwill and joy a vital part. It's higher thought and a greater plan. It's a glorious dream in the soul of man."
-Wilfred A. Peterson-

It's that time of the year when there is so much to celebrate with the yuletide spirit ringing in the air. Christmas songs are aired on the radio; everyone is busy decorating their homes and offices while the kids are waiting anxiously for Santa to make his way down the chimney with presents galore.

And what is Christmas without good food and good friends?

Christmas is celebrated in many parts of the world and each country has its own unique way of ringing in the yuletide spirit

Christmas, being international and celebrated all over the world helps to bond people of all races and languages closer. During this yuletide season, there is only one race– the human race.

What a lovely feeling!

For example, in India, its citizens decorate their houses with strings of mango leaves. Lights are then placed on the window sills and walls and a star is hung outside. A sweet holiday treat is made called *"Thali"*, and it is brought to neighbors and friends.

In England, the Christmas tree is a must-have. History reveals that the Christmas tree was made popular during the reign of Queen Victoria and Prince Albert. Prince Albert came from Germany and missed his native practice of bringing in trees to place on the tables in the house. Therefore, one Christmas, the royal couple brought a tree inside the Palace and decorated it with apples and other pretty items.

Boxing Day in England is celebrated the first weekday after Christmas and small wrapped boxes with food and sweets, or small gifts, or coins are given to anyone who comes calling that day.

The Christians in China light their homes with beautiful paper lanterns. Santa is called *"Dun Che Lao Ren."* The children hang stockings just as we do.

During Christmas, the Japanese decorate their stores and homes with greens. The only part of Christmas that they celebrate is the giving of gifts. HOTEIOSHA, the priest is like our very own Santa Claus whose tradition is to bring the children their presents.

In Singapore, the annual light up is held at Orchard Road, the town district which has several shopping centers, malls, restaurants, and 5-star hotels which make the venue popular with tourists. All shopping centers and hotels are beautifully decorated with buntings and Christmas tree lights. The President of Singapore launches the light-up in this busy downtown to give importance to this festival.

In the Philippines, Christmas celebrations begin as early as September when Christmas buntings, Christmas trees, and malls get lighted up to ring in the Christmas spirit.

I am sort of drawn into the Filipino culture having got engaged to a beautiful Filipina whose love and caring nature 'mirrors' that of my late wife, Doris. So, up goes my Christmas tree and decorations in September.

Family tradition When all of us were charting our own careers, as a closely-knit, we did lots of things together. We shared our church life together.

When it was Christmas Eve, all my brothers and I would dress to the nines and attend the midnight mass at a nearby church.

After returning home from the midnight mass, we could look forward to a sumptuous supper which our mother would painstakingly prepare.

Dad could not be present as the Club he was managing had their own elaborate Christmas celebrations.

I still remember mom's fabulous roast beef which she would cook for hours on a charcoal stove. It was a very tedious process which took as long as 6-8 hours to cook, but the final product would be absolutely fantastic! Even after several years when we got married and settled down, we would still pester mom to cook the roast beef for us. And, she gamely obliged.

After feasting on mom's crispy fried chicken, boiled friend beans and carrots, mash potatoes, roast beef, and Campbell's noodle soup with yummy French loaf, we would all join in the caroling as we caught the local Christmas TV show on the small screen.

Without fail mom would burn a row of firecrackers right on the dot of midnight and when Pat Boone's all-time classic *"Silent Night"* was aired, you could feel the Lord's presence, and it's such an awesome feeling! Celebrations at Christmas in the past were often spent with my siblings, my mom, my wife, and some of our close friends. On Christmas day, visitors would stream in at different hours of the day, and mom really had her hands full in the morning preparing yellow rice, chicken curry, mixed vegetable, salad, prawns sambal, cutlets, and fried fish.

At other times, mom and the *"gang"* would celebrate Christmas at my younger brother's flat, Frank in Serangoon Avenue.

Church brings the joys of Christmas to Doris and I Getting the community and the church to lend support to those with disabilities, as with my late wife's case who had to cope with schizophrenia for 44 years and arthritis for 10 years, helped a great deal to lift the human spirit.

During the period when Doris was alive, our Parish Church would send their church choir, numbering some 15 youths to sing carols to us in our home and present us with some gifts.

Additionally, the church would invite us together with other persons with special needs for a Christmas celebration at the church canteen where we were treated to a sumptuous meal after which we were presented with gifts and some cash. The priests would host the occasion with volunteers organizing the annual event. Certainly, the fellowship was useful to spread the joys of Christmas to one and all.

The true meaning of Christmas   Christmas should not just be all about drinking feasting and merry-making. For Christians, the most important celebration is the joy of God's love to the whole world through the birth of the Christ child – Jesus. It's an ideal time for spiritual reflection. For the lonely, poor, jobless, the homeless, and the marginalized, Christmas can be an exceptionally lonely and challenging time. More so during this COVID-19 pandemic when thousands don't even have a plate of rice to eat.

The reality is that Christmas can be a painful reminder of people's lack of happiness, joy, love, and acceptance in their lives. How do you think they feel when they witness people who are financially secure tucking in on sumptuous meals and painting the town red.

That said, let's unite the world and make inclusivity a part of the culture by inviting those who are poor to have a meal. Or send them some groceries that they help them tide over during the season. This can be done with collaborations with kind-hearted individuals or organizations.

Lend a helping and to the people of the Philippines   With 2,987 new infections reported by the Department of Health (Philippines) as of Tuesday 11th August 2020, the country's total COVID-19 case count surged to a staggering 139,538 – overtaking Indonesia which has 128,776 cases, 5,824 deaths, 83,710 recoveries as at the same date.

The Philippines will also face an additional crisis with typhoons and raging storms set to hit the country as Christmas draws near.

How will the Filipinos have the mood to celebrate this year-end festival with so much worry and anxiety on their troubled minds?

Jeepney drivers in Quezon City, Philippines, have been out of the roads since the government's lockdown of Luzon in mid-March 2020.

Without a home and livelihood for five months, some of them and their families have been living inside their jeepneys, while others beg along the roadside – come rain, come shine.

Not one who will sit and do nothing, I immediately rallied a few kind-hearted friends to raise some funds to pay for the shipment and groceries along with some used clothing to the Jeepney drivers.

I hope my goodwill gesture will spur on others to do likewise, for it's so painful for me to see and read reports of children and adults, going hungry on the hour, by the hour. For countries like the Philippines and India have thousands who are poor, sick, and undernourished.

House décor   Let's make their Christmas very special and help unite the world, as one people and one world

Besides the décor on the Christmas tree, I would hang up the Christmas cards I received from friends and family on one part of my hall by placing two sets of red ribbons from the top of the ceiling down to the floor level and then pining the cards onto the ribbons. Although E-cards are now the in-thing, I am somewhat conservative and still believe in sending out and receiving hard copies of greeting cards because they bring useful memories for years gone by.

Loving greetings @ Christmas   With the art of poetry that my readers enjoy, I take it one step further by penning personalized Christmas poems, and then choosing a suitable design to print cards. As kids love Christmas, I felt it would be good to design a child dreaming of what he wished for at Christmas. I would send such cards to my regular readers who buy our books and to the media who have published my press letters in their Forum Pages. The thinking is that if *'I remember you, you will remember me'*. That helps to build on relationships.

Christmas without my wife   During our 40 years of blissful marriage, we shared 40 Xmas celebrations. Sadly, Doris did not make it for the 41st one, where for about 2 years, I literally experienced a *"Silent Night"*. And when I heard this carol being aired on the radio on Christmas Eve, my tears fell like rain.

17th August 2014 was the date when my whole world came crashing down, for my wife whom I have taken care of for 4 decades was called to the Lord after she lost the battle with pneumonia.

But although fraught with difficulties, grieving in the first two years, the emotional pain was cushioned by caring family and friends, as well as some Good Samaritans who rallied around me and took me out for meals.

It's timely now to wish everyone *'A Merry Christmas & a Happy New Year'* as I leave you with this little Golden Nugget to ponder on, a poem which I wrote:

"Choose to love and live

When you love, you will give

When you give, you will score

And when you score, God will love you even more."

Baby's First Christmas

It's 25th December at the break of dawn
Mommy had given birth to her first newborn
Daddy's eyes sparkle with Joy
And they decided to name him – Roy

A neighbor's child who has much love
The child who is gentle as a dove
He waits patiently for me to pass by every day
Such a handsome child, so full of energy
I am so glad that this baby boy came my way

A year has quickly passed by
Oh! we all wonder how time flies
Soon, once again, it will be Christmas Day
Baby John is celebrating his first festive celebration

My wife and I are there – for we have built up healthy relations

Mom and dad, on the night before, wants to see the glow

In baby John's eyes, we all adore him – evermore

Now the parents lit up the Christmas tree

Together as friends and family,
We celebrate the Yuletide Spirit
It's for everyone to spread love, for all to see

"Merry Christmas to all children of the universe"
Put Jesus in your heart, His love must come first.

"Merry Christmas & A Happy New Year"
to one and all

By Raymond Anthony Fernando

A Nostalgic Christmas

Listening to the music of the 60s' and 70s'
The melody flowing with the breeze
Oh! How it brings back fond memories

Listening to the lyrics of Jingle Bells
A nostalgic festive season is about to begin
With joy and laughter in the air, it's so easy to tell

Watching the glow of the lights and buntings
Beautifully decorated, man it's such a lovely sight!

When Santa Claus comes down the chimney
He's greeted by none other than 5-year old Jimmy

In Christian homes
There is sheer delight
The yuletide spirit is so alive
For Christmas has arrived!

Nostalgia is ringing at the annual light up at Orchard Road

As merry makers travel to the city in buses and car loads

The brand-new clothes that parents for their children, will buy

The beautiful ladies who are somewhat camera-shy

Multi-coloured lights that stand out against the blue sky

As I look back, I can't help but wonder how time flies!

The kids are all excited!
So are those that made lots of sacrifices
Guests are served with mouth-watering dishes, wine and beer.

For Christmas is the time to bring good cheer.

By Raymond Anthony Fernando

"The principal advantage of the non-parental lifestyle is that on Christmas Eve you need not be struck dumb by the three most terrifying words that the government allows to be printed on any product: 'Some assembly required.'"

– John Leo

"Christmas Shopping: Wouldn't it be wonderful to find one gift that you didn't have to dust, that had to be used right away, that was practical, fit everyone, was personal and would be remembered for a long time? I penciled in "Gift certificate for a flu shot."

– Erma Bombeck

Leah Sanderson

Leah Sanderson grew up on Vancouver Island and moved to the Lower Mainland where she met her future husband John on the Expo Line Skytrain. Leah and John have lived in Drayton Valley since 2010 with their growing furry family-Peppy Freeway, Sally, Spirit, Charlie, Baby & Cocoa.

Leah enjoys acting and Improv and is known in the community for her performance in The Drayton Valley River Valley Players' production of the "Vagina Monologues" as the Woman Who Makes Women Happy. As well, she is an author in her own right and has written articles for the Drayton Valley Western Review, Drayton Valley Free Press, many poems and short stories, some as yet to be published.

A lover of books, and clever with words, with her creative ability she has instilled enthusiasm for the writing projects she assigns as the facilitator of Wake Up & Write! The Write Stuff, a program of the Drayton Valley Library since 2011.

Leah Sanderson *handsuponhumanity@gmail.com*

Under the Grapefruit Tree

By Leah Sanderson

Uncle Bob lay gasping in his hospital bed. I sat in the chair and leaned into him, gently holding his hand. As I had done so many times over the years, I shared with him what was on my mind.

"Hey, Uncle Bob. I came as soon as I could. It's challenging to see you like this. The family sends their love." Taking a deep breath, I launched into sharing our Christmas plans.

"An opportunity came up for us to vacation over Christmas in Nassau. A friends' sister is getting married and she suggested I take photos of the wedding. You know how I love taking pictures."

"Well, Stuart had his double lung surgery in May. It's been eight months. Seems surreal. Six months before that we were up to our eyeballs in facing his life expectancy of a few months if no surgery took place and, the stark reality that even if his pager beeps his body may reject the new lungs."

We could really use a break you know? We spoke with Stuarts' Transplant Team and they all agreed he could go on the trip.

Now we are packing a load of meds with lengthy instructions on how to manage his medications, diabetes, and who to contact at the Nassau hospital.

I squeezed his hand and rolled on.

"We maxed out our cards and booked the tickets for one week over Christmas. We'll be back on Jan 2. Stuart and I talked with the folks, his and mine. They gave their blessing. 'Go. Go and celebrate living, they said. Which struck me as odd, Uncle Bob. We are gone over Christmas and you are laying here. In hospital. No one knows if you are going to make it over the holidays.

Selfish of me I know, I want to go so badly, and yet I want to stay. I hate leaving you here. In this place. At the same time, Stuart and I need to get away. The last six months have been an emotional roller coaster for us. Heaps of stress and so many difficult but necessary conversations."

"I love you. I have always appreciated your listening ear and stories of the war. The time you brought out your Rear Air Gunner flight log. Told me of your many regrets, books enjoyed and recommended, missing your Mom in England, and teaching me to memorize Gunga Din and The Cremation of Sam McGee.

Remember the time you told me my Great Grandpa was a pirate and that a mouse lived in his leg? Or when you taught me to sing 16 men on a dead's men chest Yo Ho Ho and a bottle of rum. Drink to the devil that drunk to the rest. Yo Ho Ho and a bottle of rum.

Oh my God. I sang that for Show and Tell plus told them all about Great Grandpa.

Remember how you laughed and laughed?"

I watched the rise and fall of his chest.

Tears slid along my cheeks. I felt I was abandoning him as I left his bedside to get on that plane to the Bahamas with Stuart.

In wonder, I watched Stuart snorkel, create a costume for Junkanoo with locals, move to the primal beat of cowbells during the parade, eat fresh grapefruit from a grapefruit tree, be mistaken for a rich Doctor from Montreal by a young boy, and run into a school classmate of his younger brother in the Nassau hospital cafeteria. Our hosts thoughtfully put up a tree and took us out to a local hotel for Christmas supper. I dressed up in a Santa's Helper outfit and everyone sat on my lap and told me what they wanted for Christmas.

We were a million miles away from our families sharing an adventure of a lifetime when I learned you were gone from this world.

I sat under the grapefruit tree. Memories filled my head and my heart.

Stuart found me there. My face streaked with tears, I leaned into him, holding his hand gently.

Laughing Still

Twenty - five years
have passed
We laugh heartily
Over phone
Still

In a moment
Of glossy
Haze
Recalling
Uncooked birds

Decision made
To open presents
days in advance
We'll re-wrap
Act surprised
Christmas morn

We giggle

Wake up

No Claus

Not wanting
To admit
Disappointment

The trauma
Of a 13 yr old girl
Large box
To walnut
To $10 bill
To Wonderment

Artfully masking
present identity
From a Dad
Who knows
Always knows
What is in paper

Socks! Tie! Gloves!
Fishing lures!

Twenty -five years
have passed
We laugh heartily
Over phone
Still

Leah Sanderson

September 16, 2020

"I stopped believing in Santa Claus when I was six. Mother took me to see him in a department store, and he asked for my autograph."

— Shirley Temple

What I don't like about office Christmas parties is looking for a job the next day."

— Phyllis Diller

"People are so worried about what they eat between Christmas and the New Year, but they really should be worried about what they eat between the New Year and Christmas."

— Unknown

"Mentally I am ready for Christmas, financially I am not ready for Christmas."

— Unknown

Guy Chambers

Guy Chambers is a self-published poet. Born in Edmonton and living out at North Cooking Lake Alberta, Canada. Has two books published called "Flying Kites in the Moonlight" and "The Theater" also as eBooks. Has been published in Canada, USA, and Australia also many literary magazines like Grain, The Dalhousie Review, The Prairie Journal, Sherwood Park News, and many more.

They Say

season greeting us
snow and cold
jack frost in your faces

peace on earth that we snug up to
in blankets and coats
silent night
hoping to wake up the next morning

out there
someone said it's Christmas

socks hanging lose cold and damp
looking down at us
brick chimney decorated with hanging icicles

in the middle of the night
a man with a suit on comes around
when we are all snug in our blankets
checking to see if we are alright

out there
someone said it's Christmas

winter nowhere land
blue gray
it's another day
paying the price
nip fingers
ice crystal eyebrows

neither here or there
never understand never understood
turn out
cast out
stricken eyes
hollow bones
expressionless
unreflecting

out there
someone said it's Christmas

in the heaven
shines a bright star
neon bar light
taunting, taunting

presents wrapped in a brown paper bag
under the overcoat
angels come out of nowhere
gives us a dime or two
God bless them

others stroll by
children holding their parent's hand
staring at us
I remember these eyes
out there
someone said it's Christmas

saints in a van comes by
bearing gifts
bring cheer to dreamless eyes
gloves, toques, coats, socks

they head us to a hall
a decked hall
cheer all around
warm cozy

it's the paradise day
makeshift meal line
food only seen and smell once a year

after the pudding
back again
on the other side of the door
swept under the curb
to find
peace on the earth
snug up
in the silent night

out there
someone said it's Christmas

Old Mate

Christmas may change that what they say
as Santa thinking sending presents out on
Christmas day
through amazon because of the great rates
but you better think twice old mate
as the porch pirates will snitch them away

By Guy Chambers

Swirling Lullaby

snow resting
on the windowsill
sooth warmth
surrounding the room

glance at a child
peacefully sleeping

time at a standstill

a look of love
silent in words

teddy bear snug
soft wishes on a pillow
red suit lullaby all around

stocking of dreams
hanging close by
reindeers swirling all about

small warm heartbeat
soft fingers of hope
that can change compassion
in a heartbeat

magical castle shines
batman running in the streets
spider Mable hit the high road

grasping imagination
bringing one back
to precious time of life

By Guy Chambers

Lois Moar

Lois Moar is a writer of children's stories, erotica, and suspense. The stories, creative mixes of fact and fiction, are the result of many years of sharing her imagination and being a voracious reader.

Lois has lived across Canada and in Europe due to her husband's military career. Tom and Lois have 2 sons and 4 grandchildren.

As well as writing, quilting, and raising a family, she enjoys her beloved animals and tending to numerous plants and flowers on their acreage.

Lois is a founding member of The Write Stuff, a library program for writers since 2011.

A Remembered Christmas

By Lois Moar

The new Sears Christmas catalogue had just been delivered and my little sister Barbara and I sat on the sofa to go through it. Looking at all the wonderful toys we talked about each one and whether it was something we would put on our wish list. Every year we would look and wish for things we knew we would never get, but it was fun to make a list, a very short list, of all the things we would dream about.

While my family wasn't what was called "dirt poor" we didn't have money for frivolous things. We always had enough to eat, clothes to wear, even though most were hand me downs and there was a roof over our heads that kept us warm in the winter. At that time in our lives, my sister and I didn't really realize that we were considered poor. There were many kids we knew that weren't as well off as we were.

We knew that the kids who were considered rich would get many gifts at Christmas. They would always come to school after the holidays bragging about everything they had gotten and complaining about all the things they wanted but never got. It was hard to understand when they had so much. Sometimes it would make me sad and I would feel like I should get lots of gifts too. When asked what I had gotten for Christmas I would tell them. I remember a classmate saying "is that all you got? I would be so mad if that is all I got"

My sister and I always got a small toy, a storybook or a game, new crayons, and a cardboard cut out doll set that we could make clothes for. We would draw the clothes and then color them with our new crayons, then cut them out and fit them to the doll. There was always a new article of clothing that we needed, a blouse or a sweater and every year a new pair of woolen mitts. One year we even got new coats, not brand new, but new to us. Wearing them to church on Sunday we felt so pretty and fashionable. Another year I remember hearing Dad tell Mom that he had gotten a Christmas bonus and for her to buy us each a real doll. I wasn't supposed to have heard so I had to keep that secret to myself. Oh, how we loved those dolls.

We would wake up Christmas morning anxious to see what Santa had brought us. We each had a stocking, one of Dad's grey wool ones that we hung at the end of our beds. They would be filled with nuts, hard candy that looked like a piece of folded ribbon, and always at the top a red and white striped candy cane with a small foil-wrapped chocolate Santa beside it. The best part would be the Japanese orange in the toe of the sock. This was a wonderful expensive treat that only came out at Christmas so we only had one each. We shared them with Mom and Dad even though they said they were just for us girls. They would take just one section each to make us happy.

Dinner was always one of the best things about Christmas day. The house smelled so good with the turkey in the big blue enamel pan roasting in the oven. The sage in the stuffing added to the wonderful aroma. Every year a couple of days before Christmas Dad went out in the woods with a couple of his friends and they each shot a wild turkey for our Christmas dinner. Dad would take all the feathers off of the bird and then Mom would clean out the inside. With newspaper down on the table, Mom would put her hand inside the turkey and pull out the innards. My sister and I would kneel on chairs and lean onto the table to watch fascinated by all the yucky stuff Mom would take out. Sometimes there would be little treasures inside the turkey. One year we found a little ring with a pretty blue stone in it. Another time there was a shiny penny but most times there were just little pebbles although some of them were pretty.

With our turkey Mom always made mounds of creamy mashed potatoes from the ones that had grown in our garden. We also had peas and carrots, the green and orange looked so pretty beside the bowl of red cranberries. The table looked so colorful. Dessert was always red and green jello. It took me a few years to figure out how mom had made it so there were the two colors in the same clear glass bowl. There were always little marks on the top of the jello that we were told the reindeer had made. We never questioned just how the reindeer got in the house to walk across the bowl. A bowl of real whipped cream was served with this. Mom would use her egg beater to whip the cream into a fluffy white mound. As a child, it was fascinating to watch. Iced sugar cookies in all different Christmas shapes rounded out the meal. Mom had a very old tin cookie cutters that we used. We always had one day in December each year just for making and icing these special cookies. Friends would say that they had special pie for dessert, not plain old jello. We would just tell them that we always had pie on Sunday after the big meal. Two colored jello was special for Christmas.

After the dishes were done, we all pitched in to help, although we girls were probably more of a hindrance than a help, we would sit in the living room and listen to the Christmas carols on the radio. Dad would read us a story from one of our new books. After that Barbara and I would sit, one on each side of Mom, on the sofa as we went through the catalogue looking at all the wonderful things on the shiny colorful pages. We might not have had all the gifts that others had gotten but we knew we had something much more valuable, lots of love from our parents.

Wendy Portfors Knowler

Wendy writes a variety of genres. She has a published book titled *Remembering Love* which chronicled her journey caregiving for her husband who was diagnosed with terminal cancer. She is a contributing author to Chicken Soup For The Soul – Angels All Around book. She is currently working on an anthology and a children's book.

Wendy is a member of the Writers Guild of Alberta, Writers Foundation of Strathcona County, Millarville Church Writing Group, and Calgary Writers Group. She enjoys writing, golf, and traveling. She is remarried and resides in Turner Valley, Alberta. She enjoys hearing from fellow authors and can be contacted at or through her website www.wendyportfors.com Email: wportfors@gmail.com

The Spirit of Giving

By Wendy Portfors

I have always loved not just Christmas, but the whole season. It is a magical time of year. I grew up in Canada near the Rocky Mountains so it was never a question of whether we would have a white Christmas; it was just how much of the white stuff we would receive. Winter days are shorter and can be biting cold with plunging temperatures that make you want to curl up with a fuzzy blanket, sleepy time tea, and a great novel.

We treasure amazing views of snowcapped mountains and appreciate when the crisp air is whisked away by chinook winds that are as gentle as a mother's touch, leaving behind warm temperatures and mild days.

There is a certain aspect to fresh snow that speaks to me, calling me outdoors to make fresh footprints on the unmarked blanket of white. It is exhilarating to walk, arms outstretched, looking skyward, trying to catch drifting snowflakes on your tongue.

As a photographer it is hard to find something more spectacular than hoar frost clinging to long branches, devoid of leaves, jutting from trunks like a stick man. With the morning sun, the trees sparkle like crystals have been sprinkled along each branch.

For me, snow and Christmas go hand in hand. Everyone is busy with festivities but it is also a peaceful time of year which seems to bring out the best in people as we gather to celebrate, count our blessings and rejoice in being able to give rather than receive.

After I married, my husband and I moved from our childhood city. Being with old friends and family for Christmas just wasn't possible due to distance. As the years passed Christmas cards were replaced with Christmas letters. I would spend hours writing a letter that described all that had happened in our lives that year; the funny things, the sad times, the visitors, and the crazy weather that impacted our farm, and I always mentioned our blessings. Over the years I was able to enhance my writing with photos and the letters became a more visual recap of our life. The letters were my way of feeling connected with those that we could not celebrate with.

This year there would be no letter, no good news to share. Despite my love of everything Christmas, all the joy of the holiday season had drained from me. I could not find anything to be joyous about. It was the beginning of December and as I walked alone, I was reminded of the season at every turn with homes trimmed with colored lights that as a rule warmed my heart but now saddened me. Stores and malls were in full holiday mode with decorations and Christmas carols echoing throughout. I could not escape it no matter where I turned. Normally I would be singing as I walked through the mall, but this year was different. It was 2013 and my husband Brian had lost his battle with cancer at the end of October, just five weeks ago. I was no longer married; there was no one waiting for me at home. I now had a new title; I was a widow.

Day after day I walked aimlessly through the malls trying to get into the Christmas spirit but it did nothing for my sense of loss. I had always enjoyed shopping for presents with my husband who loved to buy items for family and friends. He was like a little kid who had no spending limit. Now I walked alone, and the joy was hard to rekindle until I heard the familiar echo of the Salvation Army bells and knew a collection kettle must be near. Not far down the mall, I saw a man dressed as Santa, with the all too familiar string of bells in his hand, that he swung rhythmically as he greeted people. His cheery demeanour instantly improved my mood. I remember my dad telling me and my siblings how important the Salvation Army had been to the troops in the Second World War. He never forgot the taste of the chocolate bars they handed out.

I opened my wallet and glanced at a five-dollar bill, but changed my mind and instead pulled out a twenty-dollar bill, which I folded and slipped into the slot on the kettle. Santa winked at me and wished me Merry Christmas.

"Merry Christmas to you," I replied before turning away. This one experience lifted my spirits and I returned home hopeful.

That evening while watching the news I was drawn to a report about the homeless in our city. For some reason, it really touched my heart. I watched the reporter interview people living on the streets and I wondered how they survived as currently, the temperature was going to dip to 30 degrees below zero Celsius that evening. It could stay that cold for weeks. The reporter commented about the constant need for warm clothing donations.

I wondered how I could help. I had been struggling to deal with my husband's clothes. Some articles I had already donated to Goodwill, but he had many items that were not good enough to be donated where they would be sold, but certainly still good enough to keep someone warm. The following morning, I called the Director at the homeless shelter. I explained my situation and told him about my husband's clothes, that I did not know what to do with. He was very comforting and told me that every piece, including socks, could be vital to someone living on the streets.

"So often our homeless are wearing boots that have been donated but are the wrong size so they must wear multiple pairs of socks to fill the boots. Believe me, all your husband's clothes will go to good use, and will be very much appreciated."

I got off the phone and had a new purpose. For Christmas, I would donate to improve the lives of those less fortunate in our city.

Over the next few days, I washed all my husband's coats, scarves, and winter wear. Then I looked in the closets and dresser and selected other pieces that I could donate. By the end of the day, I had the dining room table covered. I packaged up five large bags of my husband's clothes. Then I went shopping and purchased boxes of candy canes, individually wrapped chocolates, Christmas cookies, and some stuffed toy animals, as the

Director had told me there are many homeless children that frequent the shelter as well. It broke my heart to think of homeless children as it had never occurred to me.

The next day I woke with a renewed vision. Perhaps it was a spiritual awakening.

The shelter was in the core of the city. It was a bitterly cold day but at least it wasn't snowing. I parked in the only space which was across the street from the main door. I opened the trunk and struggled to carry two bags of clothes. As I crossed the street a man grabbed the door handle and held the door open for me. I smiled and thanked him. There was the faint odor of stale clothes. He wore faded jeans, which were too large for him, draping over his boots. I wondered why he didn't roll up the excess that was frayed and crusted with ice from dragging in the snow. Once inside I dropped the bags and almost collapsed from the weight. I mentioned my conversation from the day before to a staff member, who went in search of the Director. I retreated to unload the additional bags. Before I was done, I had unloaded 5 bags of clothes, plus the Christmas food items I had purchased. The Director appeared and thanked me for my kindness. In turn, I thanked him for helping me find a purpose for my husband's items.

As I got in my vehicle I thought of my husband's favourite Christmas movie – How The Grinch Stole Christmas. I smiled, as my heart felt like the "Grinch's", in that it grew three sizes that day!

"One of the most glorious messes in the world is the mess created in the living room on Christmas Day. Don't clean it up too quickly."

— Andy Rooney

"Be careful with drinking this Christmas. I got so drunk last night I found myself dancing in a cheesy bar... or, as you like to call it, delicatessen."

— Sean Hughes

"My mother-in-law has come round to our house at Christmas seven years running. This year we're having a change. We're going to let her in."

– Leslie 'Les' Dawson, Jr.

Tory Anne Brown

Tory Anne Brown discovered her passion for writing when she was ten years old and has rekindled her love of creation, finding inspiration for her stories in everyday life. Her story, "The Unperfect Tree," was inspired by a desire to write a Christmas story for her grandson.

She lives in Reno, Nevada, with her husband, and lives and loves to write. She blogs about her lack of a green thumb, her challenges with cooking, and has a children's corner at **www.toryannebrown.com**, and when time permits, she tweets at @ToryAnneBrown

The Unperfect Tree

By Tory Anne Brown

Each year in November after the first snowfall blanketed the forest, Farmer Jay drove up the mountain in his beat-up red pickup truck, to choose perfectly-shaped pine trees from the tree farm that was planted high in the mountains. He brought dozens of pines down the mountain to sell as Christmas trees on his lot in the city, and as was tradition, everyone came from miles around just to purchase Farmer Jay's Christmas Trees. The trees he selected had to be just the right height, shape, and color, not too big and not too little, with evenly spaced branches and lots of fresh, green, pine needles. Only trees that stood tall enough and were just the right shape, were chosen by Farmer Jay and brought down the hill to sell to families, who would decorate them with ornaments, tinsel, lights, garlands of popcorn and cranberries, and some even got homemade construction paper chains. Every year, all the pine trees vied for the honor of being chosen by Farmer Jay for the title of being a "Farmer Jay Christmas Tree."

Farmer Jay always passed up little Timmy Tree, because when Timmy Tree was a wee little pine tree, ice had fallen onto him from one of his towering relatives nearby and had broken off several of the branches on one side of his trunk. It hurt him and left him wobbly and lopsided. He stubbornly dug in his roots and grew and tried to mature evenly like the other trees, but every year the farmer drove right by him and chose the other, better, taller, straighter, trees around and behind him. Timmy Tree knew that the farmer thought the other trees were more worthy of the honor of being someone's Christmas tree. The other trees whispered their glee at being chosen and looked upon Timmy Tree with pity as they went by in Farmer Jay's beat-up red pickup truck.

When the forest animals saw what was happening, they encircled Timmy Tree in the forest clearing to discuss his problem and to make suggestions as to how he could make himself better. It seemed like everyone had an opinion about how Timmy Tree could improve himself, and with each idea, he became more dejected.

"If he would only stand up straighter!" said Sammy and Sissy Squirrel said in unison, then chuckled at each other.

The deer nodded in agreement, as did the Mallard family.

"He could wave his branches when Farmer Jay comes up the hill again," suggested Bonnie Bluebird. The Bluebird family chirped their approval of her suggestion.

"What if he made himself greener?" asked little Candy Cardinal.

Everyone laughed at Candy Cardinal's suggestion. The wolves howled and Owen, a snowy white owl, flew up to the top of Timmy Tree and perched at the top, then tried to look wise but only hooted a couple of times. Timmy Tree's body shook with sadness. His waving branches showered all of the forest animals with pine needles. Timmy Tree thought about it but saw no way to become greener. He hunched over in the Winter wind, unhappy that his friends were trying to change him into something he would never be. All the animals noticed how sad and quiet Timmy Tree had become. They crowded around him. Each of his animal friends hugged his branches and consoled him as the other trees whispered and gossiped to each other about the poor little deformed tree. Timmy Tree tried not to listen to them, but he was heartbroken anyway because he knew that Farmer Jay would never choose him to be somebody's Christmas tree.

In the middle of the discussion the forest animals were having with Timmy Tree, they heard the roar of a truck. Just then Farmer Jay drove his beat-up old truck into the clearing and spied the various animals and colorful birds that blanketed all of Timmy Tree's branches and trunk. Farmer Jay stared at Timmy Tree and the forest animals for a moment, then put his pickup in reverse and backed away from Timmy Tree, before roaring farther up the hill to where the really nice trees lived. Timmy Tree heard Farmer Jay load other trees into his pickup as the wind carried their happy voices.

Timmy Tree cried out to the farmer, "Pick me!" as Farmer Jay returned back down the hill, but Farmer Jay didn't hear him, and instead, he paused just long enough to take a picture of Timmy Tree and his friends before continuing his way down the hill to Farmer Jay's Christmas Tree lot.

After the sound of the pickup had died, leaving the forest in silence, all the animals got down off of Timmy Tree.

"Maybe next year," they tried to comfort him, but Timmy Tree was inconsolable. He sadly stood there and shed pine needles like tears as it began to snow again. The animals returned to him and tried to make him feel better. They scampered and flew up to his branches and hugged him; Barney and Betsy Bear embraced his small trunk in a warm, brown bear hug.

Suddenly there was the rumbling sound of a pickup truck that was coming up the hill. Farmer Jay was coming back! All the animals shrouded Timmy Tree's branches to protect him and all the animals and birds began talking at once. Farmer Jay's pickup entered the clearing; he brought his family up the hill to see Timmy Tree! Timmy Tree, who was busy holding all of his noisy friends, didn't pay too much attention to Farmer Jay and what he was saying.

"Do you see what I see?" Farmer Jay asked his wife and children as he pointed to Timmy Tree.

"It's the perfect tree, Daddy!" Farmer Jay's little girl, Shawna, exclaimed.

"You can't take that one!" Farmer Jay's little boy, Gabriel agreed.

Timmy Tree started to feel sad again. Farmer Jay's wife gazed at Timmy Tree in wonder.

"That white owl on the top looks like a star!" Farmer Jay's wife noted.

"See how all of the colorful animals decorate that tree perfectly? They love it! You can't take that tree!" Gabriel protested.

The family nodded in agreement as all the forest animals thronged around Timmy Tree. The other trees frowned at the attention that the little, broken tree was receiving from Farmer Jay and his family, but the animals, birds, Farmer Jay, and his family paid no attention to the other trees as they all crowded around Timmy Tree.

The animals hugged Timmy Tree, chattering to him as he hugged them back and whispered in the wind. All that winter, Farmer Jay brought his family and friends to see the special tree that all the forest animals loved. Timmy Tree stood happy and tall, knowing that he had been chosen by Farmer Jay after all, and word traveled far and wide. Every year after that, hordes of people made special Christmas holiday trips from miles around, up the mountain to see the wobbly, lopsided tree, that was graced with all of the forest animal decorations, the tree that was perfect in every way.

"I once bought my kids a set of batteries for Christmas with a note on it saying, 'toys not included.'"

– Bernard Manning

"There is a remarkable breakdown of taste and intelligence at Christmastime. Mature, responsible grown men wear neckties made of holly leaves and drink alcoholic beverages with raw egg yolks and cottage cheese in them."

– P.J. O'Rourke

"Bloody Christmas, here again, let us raise a loving cup, peace on earth, goodwill to men, and make them do the

Hi, some of you may remember me from my Boots on the Ground series and Greetings from San Diego series' in The Beacon NewsMagazine 2010-2013. For those who don't know me... My name is George Page, I am a native of Harrison Twp. Michigan. I graduated from L'anse Creuse – North and joined the USMC in 1986. I am more Marine than I am a person as I joined the Corps at 18 and served 27-years. I served in the Infantry, Combat Camera Maintenance, and Marine Corps Community Services. I served more than 8-years in over-seas posts including two tours in Iraq and one in Afghanistan.

I married a wonderful woman from Okinawa Japan, have two beautiful daughters and we have a rescue (from a South Korea dog-meat farm) Jindo/Shiba Inu Mix, Yuki Daruma (Snowball). Just before retirement, I needed to figure out life after the Corps so I completed a Bachelors degree from Southern Illinois University - Carbondale.

After retirement, I struggled to find my way in the civilian world and found a new home slinging coffee for Starbucks Coffee Co. I was a part of the veteran and military spouse hiring initiative and the face of the veteran community in San Diego for more than 5-years. However, I wanted more for my professional life after the Marine Corps.

I pursued a Masters Degree from the University of Southern California - Marshall School of Business and graduated the past May 2020. Since graduation, I work freelance as a consultant helping smaller businesses find cost savings or being the subject matter expert they don't currently have on staff. Training, travel, logistics, and supplies. We currently live in San Diego California, possibly looking for a new place to call home... tired of the riots, fires, and mudslides... Any suggestions? (probably won't move till after girls graduate High school though...)

One Marine's Evolution of Christmas

By George Page

Hello friends, I would like to share with you what Christmas has meant to me and how it has evolved over the years between my childhood and now. This is only my journey as it relates to Christmas, it may resonate with you, it may seem quite disconnected. I hope you can step into my experience and gain something from it.

I grew up in Harrison Twp Michigan, Dad's a truck driver, mom's a homemaker. Mom's mission was to make everything a fun and amazing experience for my sister and brothers. She handcrafted things, a wall calendar with small candies tied to it. One per day until Christmas day, a Well decorated home, Christmas themed knick-knacks, lights, tinsel covered tree (that we cut down ourselves from a snow-covered tree farm), with hot chocolate, hot cider, and donuts, and tractor/hay rides up and down the many rows of trees and stop or two on local snow-covered hills for some hair raising sledding!). All leading up to the inevitable Christmas countdown when local news would announce "Santa has been spotted over New York, then Cleveland, get the kiddos to bed or Santa won't come." Off to bed, we would go... Gram (maternal) lived with us on rotating Christmases, she has three daughters and close to a dozen grandchildren, she suffered from MS and was wheelchair-bound. She loved to stay with each family and get to see everyone open gifts as often as she could travel. Nana (fraternal) lived next store, of Scottish birth, she made it her mission to be engaged and share stories of her youth. Our Aunt lived not far from us so Christmas dinner alternated between our house and hers. Gifts, Felize Navidad on repeat, and games in the basement rec-room.

Mom passed from multiple cancers in 1981. Christmas 1980 was heartbreaking. We traveled to Florida where Nana had moved spent time on Ft Jefferson National Monument in the Tortuga Islands with our Uncle Ron, a park ranger there. Gramps told us he thought it might be Mom's last Christmas and he was right… Every Christmas after that was missing something…

1986 I joined the USMC and earned the title US Marine. My first Christmas away from home. I was in Infantry Training School in Camp Pendleton. I was welcomed into the home of my cousin's in-laws for the day, dinner, and conversation, and quite a few beers which led to phone calls home and plenty of tears before it was back to base the following day.

It would be several years before I went home for Christmas again. It was great to be with family. But it was never the same without mom, then Gram and Nana Gramps were in Florida. I married a woman from Okinawa. Spending quite a few Christmases there was different… Christmas was not as big to her and her family, no tree, no major decorations a small gift or two, and a nice dinner that evening. I watched it expand in her eyes as she loved and moved around the world with me.

Our first daughter was born in Nov 2004 within 25-days of her birth I was sent to Iraq and spent her first Christmas in Fallujah. Now she was only weeks old and has no recollection of it. But, it was one of many a "milestone" missed in the life of my child during my active service.

Christmases began to build into those of my youth as my wife wanted the girls to have the best of everything. No matter where we were we found a tree we had an artificial tree for a few years that we picked up after a move or during an after Christmas clearance sale. We welcomed a second daughter in March of 2007 it would be 2009 when we arrived in California before we went to a farm to find a live tree to experience the smells of pine in the house decorate the tree and do more traditional type things of games and Christmas themed movies each night as we got closer and closer to Christmas. Charlie Browns Christmas, Frosty the Snowman, Rudolph the Red-Nosed Reindeer, (Burl Ives, Jimmy Durante, Boris Karloff or Fred Astaire narrated) It's a Wonderful Life, Christmas Story, Miracle on 34th St… all the classics with a handful of newer favorites as well. The Nightmare Before Christmas, Scrooged, and The Santa Clause series thrown in for good measure.

No matter where we were in the world Christmas was celebrated sometimes with family, sometimes without blood relatives. Extended military families and friends Huge amounts of food, from traditional family recipes of Roast Beast, Yorkshire pudding, Turkeys (smoked, deep-fried, or oven-baked) Yams, Green Bean Casserole, Garlic Smashed potatoes, to Japanese favorites Sushi, egg roll, Yakisoba, fried rice, with desserts of mochi, and traditional Pumpkin, Apple, Pecan pies or Apple Crisp with Vanilla Ice cream.

Throughout the years, the myriad changes in life circumstances place lived or endured. Christmas was ALWAYS meaningful, always shared, and will always be.

Merry Christmas my Friends ----- *George, Kumiko, Namika & Sora Page*

My name is Jennifer Dales but when writing I go by Jen Dales as that is what I am most was commonly known as. I am 33 years old, married with a little girl.

I have been writing since I was 13 --started with poetry and now I've written a few postcard stories (under 1000 words) and some short stories too. I have written some children's poetry as well.

I love to read and write. I once was in an amateur dramatics society and I love to sing, just not in public anymore. I like to spend lots of time with my family and friends. I would love to have my poetry published in a book and also have a couple of short story collection books: one children's one and one adult one. If I published more that would be amazing but those are the important ones to me.

I love everything about Christmas and believe there are lots of different sides to Christmas as you will see in my poems below. Charles Dickens wrote about the three ghosts of Christmas and I am writing about the three sides of Christmas.

The harshness of winter – Blizzard
The magical feeling of closeness – Parisian Christmas
The fun, whimsical childlike element of Christmas – Christmas Rule.

Blizzard

Through the window, the sky is dark
And yet the night hasn't even begun
The clock strikes six
Frost-covered roofs and snow-covered trees
Is enough to make our body freeze.

One wishing to be sitting by the fire
The heat from the hot blaze keeping them warm
and a hot chocolate in their hand with marshmallows on top.
They're all snug like a bug on the rug
Reading a fantastic poem
Tears flood their eyes.

Thinking of those poor souls
Still lost, trying to find their way home
Surprised no-one's gotten frostbite from the cold.
With temperatures below five degrees
One can't believe they're stuck in the middle
Of one of the worst winters blizzards.

People wait by the phone
For news to come
But nothing, not even one
Crying that one of their own is hurt.
The phone rings
Sighs of relief, the blizzard has gone
Everything is going to be fine.

Parisian Christmas

On this starry night
under the light of the moon;
I see in a distance
My fairy-tale dream come true.

As the snow gently falls
I glide over to the place
where we agreed
to meet one day.

Under the lights
of the Eiffel Tower;
I meet my mystery man there
to start our happily ever after.

the midst of this
Parisian Christmas wonderland;
we pledge our lives together
as we wed and say 'I do'.

Let this be a Christmas to remember.

By Jennifer Dales

Christmas Rule

Santa's elves running around in the workshop
Making toys for little girls and boys
On the night of Christmas Eve.
Santa and his eight reindeer friends
Fly around high in the sky
Throwing toys down children's chimneys.
Stocking's placed above the fireplace
Filled with lots of Christmas treats.
Now that Santa's job is done
Off he goes into the night shouting;
"Now Dasher, now Dancer, now Prancer, now Vixen
On Comet, on Cupid, on Donner and Blitzen."

The next morning one awakes
To find lots of wonderful goodies Santa's left behind
But what does one leave in return
Does one send him a letter saying "Thank You"
Or does one forget all the work they have done?

So remember boys and girls
This year let's not be rude
And send them something
Showing them of one's gratitude
I'm sure they would glad
But remember what we say ;

"To give, one will receive
And to get, one must give away."

So now everyone knows the
Christmas Rule
A jolly, jolly good day to all.

By Jennifer Dales

Stella Croning

Stella Croning is a retired Health Care Professional. An author of a short novella, as well as an anthology, and several unpublished stories and poems, she has a passion for writing.

Animals have always been a part of her/her son's lives and love for them comes naturally. Her sons Ralph and Wayne state "Mom would rather go hungry herself rather than see an animal starve; she would cater to our pets first, which included all critters from cats, dogs, birds, an injured crow, and yes, an old abandoned donkey!"

Stella now lives in Winnipeg, Canada, and spends as much time as she can with her two grandchildren and their pet cat 'Logan'. Hope you enjoy her poem.

A CHRISTMAS POEM

By Stella Croning

A little boy, his age just four,
Looks towards the neighbours open door,
With wistful look and eyes so bright
At a Christmas Tree adorned with lights.

Oh, what thinks he, as he looks on?
That little face so all forlorn?
Does he look round that Christmas Tree?
Laden with gifts from shopping sprees?

Oh, wonder what his heart desires
His eyes alight with hidden fires,
All lost in thought that little mind,
With longings, wishings of all kinds.

Then sudden laughter spoils his thoughts,
His wishings have all gone about,
He looks on unaware of tears,
That roll on as the midnite nears.

Oh, brother look around and see,
Make sure no child sadly sees your tree,
Make sure no tears are in his eyes,
With longing's deep that hide inside.

Somewhere, there are many a-children,
who never have seen a tree a-laden,
Take one wrapping, keep aside,
For a wishful boy
Who somewhere abides.

"This past Christmas, I told my girlfriend for months in advance that all I wanted was an Xbox. That's it. Beginning and end of list, Xbox. You know what she got me? A homemade frame with a picture of us from our first date together. Which was fine. Because I got her an Xbox."

– Anthony Jeselnik

"There are some people who want to throw their arms round you simply because it is Christmas; there are other people who want to strangle you simply because it is Christmas."

– Robert Staughton Lynd

Michelle M. Levise

Enjoy all that makes you happy. This comes from a woman who was beginning her Golden Years. Deciding that I needed more enjoyment in my life and realizing the only obstacle preventing it from happening was me.

Thus, I began making changes. Changes that involved my love of the arts. Just thinking of the many possibilities seemed as though a door was opening that had been locked some years ago. I began to feel the passion for my dreams. I was finally allowing myself to create something of beauty. Something that would benefit others and myself. I am now in the process of restoring a historic home that is one hundred seventy - seven years old. Within it, there exists, the inner sanctum, a studio that allows my passion to reveal itself with paint on canvas. Melodic words making way for a song.

Stories told with grace and honor. My favorite of all is early morning at twilight to catch the rays from the sunrise with my camera. I so love returning to my studio viewing pictures of what was taken just moments before. These are truly my Golden Years and I am filling them with precious moments and all that makes me happy.

Sarah's Santa

By Michelle M. Levise

Christmas proved to be only days from arrival, as each day was crossed off the calendar. It was a constant reminder of how quickly Sarah's time was growing short in making their Christmas, the best it could be.

Living on a shoe-string budget and making ends meet had become a way of life, for Sarah, since her husband abandoned her and their children. Her priorities were her two precious little girls who delighted in the thought that Santa was coming to visit their home. Determined, she was going to make sure, her girls, would not go without.

Sarah was a strong-minded, young lady, keeping promises, fulfilling obligations, and being the best mom, she could possibly be meant everything to her. Strong-willed and with the best of intentions she formulated a plan. Not foolproof but possible.

Christmas was soon to arrive, and it felt more like something to dread. She had barely enough money to live week to week. How would she manage to provide a Christmas for her children? It was the end of the week all the bills were paid. They had enough food for the following week and fifteen dollars leftover.

Having promised the girls a real Christmas tree, they left for the tree lot.

Arriving with her girl's hand in hand they began their search through rows and rows of Evergreens, Cedars, Pines, and Firs. Glistening with a light dusting of snow the trees appeared so beautiful as if dressed in white crystal coats of snow and ice. This was truly a highlight of their day. Finally, it was beginning to feel like Christmas, as the scent of fresh pine filled the air.

Anxiously, Sarah searched for a tree that was within her means. The money Sarah had seemed minuscule and hardly enough to purchase a tree. All the trees were priced at more than what she could afford. Saddened, she gathered the girls and explained that this year they would not be able to have a Christmas tree. Feeling like she had failed they headed toward the car.

Unexpectedly and only moments before leaving, the sound of jingle bells rang out from within the trees. Turning to see where the sound came from stood a man with, snow-white hair, red suspenders, and a red ball cap. He was gesturing them to come to him. As they approached, he asked them if he could be of help. The girls excitedly told him that their mom was sad that she could not buy them a Christmas tree. Informing him "She only has fifteen dollars/' Then with a smile that lit up his twinkling eyes he replied, "I have the perfect tree, and it's just fifteen dollars." Sarah knew that he was taking a loss, but the promise she made to her girls helped her swallow her pride and accept the gentle man's offer.

Happily, he chose a most beautiful tree, trimmed it to perfection, carefully bundled it, and placed it in the trunk of her car. He then accepted the fifteen dollars and turning to Sarah's children gave the money to the girls with explicit instructions, "You go buy your mother a Christmas present, something special." The girls were tickled that they could now buy their momma a present.

Sarah was so thankful for this kind man's generosity. She felt as if there was something ever so special about him. After helping the girls into the car, she turned to thank him. He was nowhere to be found. Only the sound of jingle bells again resumed from the trees. Her girls wanted to know where the nice man was. Sarah explained that he was a busy man and had to help other people in need. All the while believing he was the true spirit of Christmas.

Sarah's story took place twenty-three years ago. Soon after that Christmas, she became quite successful in her career and could afford to provide her children with whatever their needs were.

The following year Sarah and her girls returned to the Christmas tree lot to purchase a tree. There standing among the evergreens was the man with a smile and twinkling eyes, with white hair, red suspenders, and a red ball cap every Christmas since, a tree graces Sarah's home from a kind, gentle man's tree lot. Yes, you know the one! Red ball cap, smiling eyes and sells Christmas trees from his lot ••.there is something special about his trees, they just seem to twinkle.

Merry Christmas and may all your Christmas trees twinkle...and if they don't go see the fella wearing a red ball cap, surrounded by evergreens, at the tree lot.

GIFTS OF THE SPIRIT: PRICELESS

By Michelle Marie Levis

Holidays, such as Christmas, are especially known for the joys of family and friends. Time well spent, with loved ones, reminiscing past gatherings. Carols, the breaking of bread, stories, laughter, and sweet sentiments of giving. More importantly, to come together and reflect with honor and respect, the greatest gift of all, the blessed birth of the Christ child. The child that taught us about love and giving, the true meaning of Christmas.

Through the years, I have kept Christmas cards of well-wishing, little gifts of caring words penned on paper, photos of family gatherings, and celebrations with friends. Little keepsakes of all shapes and sizes, all a reminder of happy times. Meaningful and loved, I have kept these treasures in a safe and protected place. WORTH: Priceless.

Each item represented an expression of love. Trinkets that perhaps had no value to someone else, such as, a tiny plastic clown that came from a Cracker Jack box. A gift from my son when he was a little boy because he knew how I loved clowns. I carried that little clown in my wallet for years. Eventually, it found its way into my special place of memories. Little gifts are given from the little hands of a child, who gave from his heart. WORTH: Priceless.

Within my inner sanctum sat a gift box, tied with a blue satin ribbon. The box contained hand-penned love letters from the love of my life. Some letters were written during wartime. The holidays would come and go, but his written word remained tucked within the branches of our Christmas tree. This was the man who looked at me as if I were the most beautiful girl in his world. His precious words always made their way back home to me. Letters that encouraged our wills to remain strong; 'til we meet again'. WORTH: Priceless.

Oh yes, my treasury was filled with memories of loved ones. Cards with sentiments of joyful wishes came with the births of our children. Wishes for happiness came with each passing year in celebration of getting older. All kinds of expressions are placed on paper wishes for well-being along with Christmas greetings. Some from friends that we had not heard from all year. Always a joy to receive. Always a joy to remember. WORTH: Priceless

Lest we not forget the ever so valuable, 'Gifts of the Spirit'. The unity of Family love, love of country, Faith made realistic, Hope for the future, complete trust in God, and Thanksgiving. These though formless are treasures of the heart and soul. With the application, they will take on a form in time. These are a treasure trove of gifts that keep on giving and are made manifest from the Lord our God.

WORTH: Precious beyond anything you can imagine.

So, my dearies, my sacred place is full of memories, and each and everyone has a story to tell. All are kept in a safe and loved place. A place that helps me remember just how loved I am. My wish for you is that you will keep safe and protect the memories that remind you just how loved you are. WORTH: Priceless.

Merry Christmas

"Once again, we come to the Holiday Season, a deeply religious time that each of us observes, in his own way, by going to the mall of his choice."

– Dave Barry

"Ever wonder what people got Jesus for Christmas? It's like, 'Oh great, socks. You know I'm dying for your sins, right? Yeah, but thanks for the socks! They'll go great with my sandals. What am I, German?'"

– Jim Gaffigan

Elizabeth Williams

Elizabeth Williams is a novelist and poet. Before becoming a full-time writer, she worked in the public sector for many years.

She now lives in South East London with her husband, young son, and a rescue cat named Blaze.

Christmas Drinks

By Elizabeth Williams

The rain wasn't exactly seasonal, Meg thought as she pushed open the doors of the bar. It was cold though, and the temperature change as she went inside made her feel sweaty and flushed. She quickly took off her leather jacket and slung it over her arm as she scanned the room. No sign of him. He must be out the back.

She glanced around the space, taking in the fairy lights strung across the banisters of the wide staircase that led to the upper bar, and the paper lanterns hanging from above. Despite the dominant mock baroque look, all dark wood, and purple crushed velvet, the designers had left the ceiling of the bar exposed, with the pipes on display. The meeting of industrial metal and carved wood was the ultimate paradox, perhaps.

She couldn't imagine Matthew up there on a step ladder putting up the decorations himself. He must have got some of the younger staff to do it. Perhaps that new one - she looked like an art student. They all adored him, so they would do whatever he wanted.

Meg weaved through the tables to the bar to get a drink. It was still pretty early, but it was a Friday in December and the after-work crowd was gradually transforming into the groups who were in it for the long haul. She could see people looking at their watches and frowning, trying to work out if they could get away with one more drink. A man next to her was furiously tapping a message into his mobile phone. Texting the wife, she thought wryly, as she caught Ieuan's eye at last.

"Pinot please, darling. A big one!" She barely needed to tell him, really, since she was here so often and never varied her order. But it was part of the routine.

"You after the boss?" Ieuan asked, in his lilting Welsh accent, as he poured the golden liquid into the measuring cup.

"Oh, Matthew? No, not especially. Just meeting some friends later, maybe. Wouldn't go anywhere else, you know!" She tapped her card on the reader. "Is he around?" she added, as casual as she could manage.

"Upstairs in the office."

Meg's mind flitted to the night a couple of weeks ago when she'd come to the bar after closing. He'd taken her up to the office and locked the door. She remembered his hands on her body and the smell of his skin. Her face didn't betray her thoughts though, of course, and Ieuan chattered on happily.

"He said he had to make some phone calls. Been some cock up with the order from the brewery, he's in a right tizz about it. Can't be running out of beer now, can we?" There were a few people leaning up against the bar, so he wandered off and turned on his winning smile for the next customer, a middle-aged woman who giggled slightly ridiculously while he flirted with her as he made her cocktail order.

Taking a sip of her drink and savoring the crisp, cool sensation in her mouth, Meg made her way over to an empty table. The crowd had thinned out a bit since she arrived, the calm before things started to hot up again later. The sound system was playing the usual Christmas tunes, the volume not cranked up to full-on Friday night volume yet. She sat down, plonked her bag on the seat next to her, and rummaged around for her work notebook.

Matthew always said she was mad, trying to work in the bar. Of course, she couldn't bring anything out of the hospital that related to patients, but there was always studying to do, thinking through cases, planning, and making notes. She tugged out a battered photocopy of a journal article she'd been carrying around for weeks, never having found time to read it. She focused easily. All those years of night shifts and studying for exams meant she could concentrate anywhere.

"All work and no play, love?" A voice broke her concentration and she looked up, to see a tallish, bald man leaning against her table. He was wearing a football top and slurping a pint of lager. "Want to join us?" He motioned across the bar to a group of men crowded around a table, which was groaning with empties.

Meg smiled as neutrally as she could manage. "Thanks, but I'm waiting for someone," she said, turning back to her papers and hoping he would go away. She found in these situations that being pleasant and bland, the way she sometimes was with unhappy patients, usually did the trick, and she was right. He took the hint and disappeared off to rejoin his mates.

Her focus was gone, though, for now at least. She sat back and took another swig of her wine, looking around the bar but studiously averting her eyes from the direction of the bald man's table.

It was mainly office workers, she surmised, watching the group nearest to her. The women were in glittery blouses and pencil skirts and the men were either in suits, with top buttons undone and ties loosened or sweltering in Christmas jumpers. The Fairytale of New York came on the sound system and a couple of the women slung their arms around each other and started to sway, bellowing along to the track, tuneless but joyful all the same.

Doctors' nights out were never like that anymore. Not since the student days. Now their Christmas parties were black tie, in over-priced hotel conference suites, organized in August or September by earnest secretaries with spreadsheets. Most people had to drive, so only one person out of each couple could get drunk, and it always felt a bit awkward and imbalanced.

It was raining hard outside now, and a gang of students crowded in through the door, dripping as they pushed their way to the bar. It would be the end of term soon, then the locals would take over again. Meg watched the girls order their Bacardi Breezers and strip off their coats, revealing identical denim shorts over tights and strappy tops. She glanced down at her own outfit – black skinny jeans and polo neck, no jewelry, hardly any makeup. True, she didn't have time for fashion, but she wasn't that interested either. And Matthew certainly didn't seem to care.

He still hadn't told her about Christmas. Not that it made any difference. She'd told her parents she was working, months before she'd even got the rota. She couldn't face another Christmas in their stifling house. The endless jibes at her sister, who may or may not turn up, and may or may not bring her long-suffering girlfriend, to be exposed to their subtle but omnipresent homophobia. And in the evening, the TVs blaring on different channels in each room as her mother and father refused to watch the same program.

No, as far as they knew, she was on-call over Christmas. At least they had something to tell their friends, in the supermarket and in church. Their heroic daughter, saving lives over Christmas. In truth, she'd volunteered to cover Christmas Day but they hadn't needed her, so she had plans for a lie-in, a chicken supreme pizza, and a Netflix binge. She knew by now not to expect anything of Matthew.

She turned back to her paper and picked up where had she left off, scribbling notes in the margin and thinking about how she could present it to the medical students at the next journal club. The content was too dense to do justice to in twenty minutes, but she could summarize the important bits and the keen ones could follow it up with her at their teaching session.

She suddenly felt her skin tingle; she sensed him watching her. She forced herself to count to ten, then glanced up to see him standing halfway down the open staircase, a smile playing on his lips as he looked down at her. He wouldn't come straight over, she knew that. He headed for the bar and served a crowd of waiting girls, laying on the charm as usual. She looked down again as she saw him pouring out a glass of wine and carrying it in her direction.

"On the house," he murmured, setting it down on the table in front of her.

She looked up and smiled. "Sit?"

"Just for a minute," he said, sitting down next to her. He reached under the table and ran his hand up her thigh. "You look nice."

"I look the same as always," she replied. "Don't see why I should make any effort for you, when you never, ever call me."

"Why should I call, when I know you'll be here when I need you?"

Despite herself, her stomach flipped as she saw the look in his eyes. What was it about him that made her insides turn into slush? Like wet snow on the pavements, in this city where it never stopped raining. What they had wasn't beautiful and clean, like fresh snow. It was darker, and just as dangerous as black ice when it froze solid.

"Christmas. Are you working?" he asked, suddenly serious.

"Don't know, shift swaps aren't all finalized yet." It was better to be evasive, she thought, until she knew what he was getting at.

"Well, Amelia's going to visit her folks. I'm not, but this lot think I am." He waved his hand vaguely in the direction of the bar.

She looked up at him in surprise, knowing better than to ask any questions, but feeling her heart rate increase. Seeing him hesitate, uncharacteristically, she silently willed him on. *Keep talking, Matthew, keep talking.*

"Trial separation, her idea. She's fed up with me working all the time." He took a deep breath, exhaled slowly. "So, Christmas. Think about it." He stood up, leaned down, and whispered in her ear. "Buy something red, leave the door unlocked. I know you'll be there when I need you."

She watched him cross the floor, stopping to chat with the customers as he went. Emperor of all he surveyed. She stared out of the window at the lights on the High Street. Outside the temperature must have dropped. The rain had turned to sleet.

James (Jamie) Peter Cortez

James (Jamie) Peter Cortez, of Las Vegas, passed away August 16, 2019. He was born May 30, 1962, in Henderson and resided in Southern Nevada his entire life. Jamie was a teacher at Robert Taylor ES in Henderson and a Producer/Director/Administrator at KLVX Channel 10. Jamie served his community as an Educator and Administrator for the Clark County School District, foster parent, and youth soccer coach.

He was an amazing man and an equally amazing story-teller and poet. He has always been an incredible inspiration to his family and friends, and his stories continue to inspire.

The Christmas Miracle

By Jamie Cortez

"It was Christmas Eve!" was the first thought as my eyes opened. It was a dreadful year. My Dad was sick from cancer. I can tell that he and my Mom are very scared.

My Dad has to go to the hospital for a week every month for chemo. My Mom told me that the chemo would make Daddy better; but first, it had to make him sick. I am not sure why medicine would make someone sick if they are making them better.

After coming home from the hospital all he did was throw up. It made me scared to see him throwing up all the time. He was the strongest man I knew and now, well now, he was skinny and bald.

We had to move out of our house because without Dad's check, we couldn't pay for it anymore. We had to move to an apartment a couple of months ago.

My Mom says that he is getting better all the time; but, I don't see it. It is kind of weird to miss someone who is around you. I miss when he played football with me and I miss him when he is too sick to help me with my homework. I even miss him when he is sleeping in his chair. He sleeps in his chair a lot.

I didn't know how to help him so I wrote Santa a letter telling him what I wanted for Christmas.

"Dear Santa, All I want for Christmas this year is for my Dad to be healthy again. I have been very good this year. I don't want any toys. I will play with last year's toys if I can just have my old dad back. ~Tommy."

I wasn't sure that he had gotten the letter. My second-grade teacher, Mrs. Harvey told our class that letters need to have a mailing address so the mailman would know where to send it. I don't know where Santa lives except that it is at the North Pole. So, I put that on the envelope.

All I could think of throughout the day was Santa and my Dad. I really wanted my dad to be better and Santa was the only person I could think of to help him.

By the afternoon, I had a plan. I would go to the mall and see him. I know they always want money for that Santa but I promised that I would only be a minute.

"You can't see Santa without a ticket, little boy," said the elf.

I started to cry. I really didn't mean to cry but I had been waiting in that line for over an hour and when I was so close to him that I could almost touch him. I looked at the ticket line and the tears flowed.

Santa started stressing that a kid was crying in his line so he told me to go up there. I walked to him and whispered in his ear. "Santa, can you help my Dad? He has cancer and my Mom is so scared that he will not become better. Santa, I can hear her crying at night; but, I pretend that I am sleeping. He is a really nice man. He always gives money to the old man next to the freeway. I just want the chemo to work for him. Can you help?"

Santa looked at me. I saw a tear form in his eyes as he said, "Tell me your name, son."

I looked at him, "Santa, you don't remember me? My name is Tommy. Tommy Rivers."

"Of course I know you, Tommy. I have seen so many children today. I-I-I am sorry."

I was worried that he wasn't the real Santa. I was watching a race in Las Vegas where they had over seven thousand "Santas" running. Maybe he was one of the "running" kind.

Throughout dinner, I tried to smile; but, my Dad kept asking me if I was feeling alright.

As I am lying in my bed thinking of my Dad and Santa and how things are going to be after Christmas, I heard a sound on the roof. My eyes got as big as saucers as I sat up in my bed.

I heard the doorbell. I was confused. Santa doesn't ring the doorbell.

The voices of people downstairs and the laughing and the bells and the "Ho Ho Ho's" made me sit up in my bed. I got up and looked down the hall. There were people bringing packages and food. My Mom was just staring at them as came into our apartment.

My Dad even came to the door. He never goes to the door for anything. He doesn't even answer the phone anymore. He seemed to know everyone who had a package.

When all the packages, presents, and food were brought in, they all sat in every seat in the house. In fact, there were people sitting on the floor. I never remembered seeing a "grown-up" sitting on the floor.

 Then, I heard the noise on the roof again.

"Ho Ho Ho!" came from the front door.

There was a man in a red suit that came to the door carrying a bag.

"Who is Tommy?" asked Santa. "I got a letter from a Tommy from this house." He pointed at people who were staring at him throughout the room, asking if they were Tommy.

I finally said, "I am Tommy."

"You are the boy who wrote me the letter that said that he didn't want any toys? Well, Sonny, I HAVE to give you something…"

Before he could finish, I yelled, "But I don't want any toys, I just want my Dad to feel better."

My Dad said, "I couldn't feel any better than right now, Tommy. It seems everyone I love is here, there is no better gift than that."

Santa whispered something to me that only I could hear, "Tommy, love is what is going to get your Dad through this. He is the strongest person I will see tonight. You are the source of his strength. Please, Tommy, let me give you a present."

I hadn't thought of anything so I just said the first thing that popped into my mind, "I want a new fishing pole so me and my Dad can go fishing when he feels better."

"Here," he said as he got a present from the bag. "Merry Christmas." was all he said. On the tag was written, "Tommy".

I don't know how he knew about the letter if he wasn't the REAL Santa. I don't know how he knew I was going to ask for a fishing pole. I didn't even know until it came out of my mouth. I don't know how he knew that my Dad was going to get better; but, he knew it all.

When anyone says that they don't believe in Santa, I know that Santa believes in them, and isn't that what Christmas is all about?

I've had this look for about a year. I usually grow this beard out around Christmas. I like to go to malls dressed as Jesus, and I like to then walk around the mall and go, 'No! No! This wasn't what it was supposed to be about, people!'

Then if there's a Santa I've had this look for about a year. I usually grow this beard out around Christmas. I like to go to malls dressed as Jesus, and I like to then walk around the mall and go, 'No! No! This wasn't what it was supposed to be about, people!'

Then if there's a Santa at the mall, I walk up to him and say, 'Listen, fat man, you're just a clown at my birthday party.'"

– Marc Maronat

Christina Torres

My name is Cristina Torres I have self-published my first book titled Seven Deadly Sins. It has positive reviews on Good Reads and Amazon. It is book one of my Christian Horror series. I have finished the second part of that book and hope to have it published soon. I have also started a children's series. I have published a few short stories and poems in a community newspaper Highgrove Happenings.

I have collaborated on other books and have written eulogies and poems. I enjoy crafts and making my own handbags in my spare time. I have worked as a librarian assistant and motivated consultant. I love to travel and meet people.

Doctor Vlad Cooper

By Cristina Torres

It was a snowy evening in the town of Mezbeth. The town is a small community of fishermen, woodsmen, and a few business professionals that either worked in town or took a bus to the next town. Anything exciting rarely occurred in such a small town. The people that lived in the community were not very welcoming to strangers or visitors. Everyone kept to themselves living the same daily routines day after day night after night. Nothing unusual ever occurred. The homes in the town were crafted of the mighty oak trees that grew in the forest. The streets were covered in pavement and the street lights adorned every neighborhood. Every now and then some of the light bulbs would flicker, but the residents never bothered to exchange the bulbs. Some bulbs would remain at the base until they are completely burnt out because nobody wanted to inconvenience the electrician in town to replace the bulb.

The people in the community are hardworking people who only live for themselves and have a strict motto "Do not inconvenience anybody" it is a rather strange motto that they live by. Everyone in town swore by that oath, that is until one day an unusual visitor stopped by.

Freshly fallen snow covered the edge of the entrance to a trail that led to the town of Mezbeth. The weather is consistently changing. It would rain. It would snow and on occasion, it would be windy. It was 6:00 am and the only bus that would pass near Mezbeth that morning was running late. There are only a handful of people that ride the bus into the neighboring town that was about one hundred miles away. The people in the community use a trolley to get to the main road that is closed to all outsiders.

"It's fifteen minutes past six." Said a short lady holding a flower pattern canvas bag.

Another man looked at his watch and agreed with the woman named Mildred. "You are absolutely right Mrs. Mildred." He is a stocky fellow with a tan suit and matching tie. He is holding a black briefcase and paper bag in his hand.

"What shall we do? We're all going to be late" Said Miss Peterson, Miss Peterson is a tiny woman with short hair and wears glasses. She is dressed in a white dress with purple flowers. She is holding her purse and keeps glancing at the road. Thomas the man with the black briefcase smiles towards her and stays quiet.

There is another man standing nearby. He is a short stubby elderly man. He is wearing a black suit and has reading glasses around his neck hanging on a chain and a pair of bifocals in his shirt pocket sticking out. "I see no reason for the bus to be running late!" he shouts

Mildred looks at the man. "Raymond, in all my years this is the first time the bus is late."

"I'm sure there's a logical explanation." Said Thomas

The trolley driver looks at his watch and turns the vehicle on.

"Billy!" shouts Raymond you can't be seriously leaving us here. What if we missed the bus and need to return to town?"

Billy looks at them briefly and sighs. "I can't wait around here all day waiting for you all to make up your minds on what to do." Just as Bill was about to drive off he hears Mildred shouting "It's here, it's here."

The bus moves swiftly down the road Raymond, Thomas, Mildred, and Mrs. Peterson walk closer to the bus stop and wait eagerly for its arrival. Billy feeling eager and rather curious gets down from the trolley and walks slightly to the bus stop. He stands there with a curious expression. The bus gets closer and starts to slow down slightly. The screeching sounds of the brakes are too loud that Billy tries to cover his ears and nods his head in disbelief. The bus makes a halting stop after the bus sign. Mildred, Mrs. Peterson, Thomas, and Raymond begin walking fast towards the bus. Billy follows them from behind.

Raymond being annoyed begins to shout at the bus driver. "What's the meaning of making us walk past the bus sign!"

"I don't think the driver can hear you!" shouted Mildred

Raymond with a serious expression turns to look at Mildred. "I didn't ask for your opinion

Thomas shouts "We're all running late, we should tell the driver he needs to drive faster to make up for the lost time. Wouldn't you agree Mrs. Peterson?"

She looks down at her watch and nods her head. "This is ridiculous, why isn't he opening the door?'

"I can't see the driver," said Raymond

"Is he even on the bus?" asks Mrs. Peterson

Raymond begins to pound on the door. "Open the door, were late as it is. Thomas don't just stand there. Help me pry the door open."

"Why would you inconvenience me? I would have to put my artifact down."

"Don't be naïve. This situation affects us all."

Thomas moves closer and begins to try to pull the doors apart.

"Billy I hope you know how to drive a bus?" said Mrs. Peterson

Billy with the surprised assumption replies. "I'm no bus driver."

"If you can drive a trolley, then you can drive a bus." Said Mildred

"Maybe you didn't hear me. I have never driven a bus."

"Then today is your lucky day. It is never too late to learn." Said Mrs. Peterson sarcastically

"Madam, that would inconvenience me. I have a job to do and lingering here with you all has made me late."

"I agree with Mrs. Peterson if you can drive one vehicle, then you can drive anything. It shouldn't be too complicated for you."

"My dear Mildred has it not occurred to you, that I have prior obligations."

"Will you two leave Billy alone!" Shouted Raymond "We still have to see if the bus driver is on the bus." Feeling frustrated Raymond stops trying to pull the doors apart. "Thomas maybe you should walk around the back to see if the driver is on the bus."

"Alright, if I must" Thomas walks slowly towards the back of the bus and begins to hear voices coming from inside. He hears a loud screeching sound and closes his eyes slightly. He gets closer and sees the back door opening. He begins to hear Raymond shout "Well is the driver back there?" Thomas looks straight ahead and sees a hand covered in blood push the door open. He stops slightly and sees blood dripping on the ground.

"What's taking you so long? Is the driver there?" Shouts Raymond

"I think you better come back here and take a look!" shouts Thomas

Raymond looks at Mildred and Mrs. Peterson "You two better stay here." Raymond walks towards Thomas and sees the puddle of blood on the ground.

"What do you suppose is going on?' asked Billy

"Billy, who told you to follow us? Why on earth would you leave the ladies alone? Asked Raymond

"I want to see for myself."

Thomas gets closer to the door and sees the bloody hand being raised slightly.

"What do you see Thomas? Whispered Raymond

Billy sees the bloody hand dripping and turns back.

"Where are you going? Asked Raymond nervously

Thomas hears the mumbling voices getting louder. "What's going on?" asked Raymond from behind in a low whisper

"I think it's an argument."

"Well don't just stand there confront them."

Angrily Thomas turns around and looks at Raymond. "And just what am I suppose to say?"

"Anything just do it."

"This is a mistake, what if they get angry that I interrupted?"

"We need to know what's going on."

"Then you go!"

"Me!" shouts Raymond

"Yes! This is your idea."

"Fine!" Raymond walks around to the door and sees the bus driver. With a shocked expression, he asks "Are you alright?"

The bus driver sitting and the edge of the platform lift his arm a bit higher. He looks at Raymond and says "I'll be all right. The doctor says it's not that serious."

Thomas comes around towards the back and sees the bus driver sitting. "What happened?

Raymond looks inside the bus and sees a man coming towards them with a black bag.

"Good morning." Said the man

"Doctor," said the bus driver with a concerned look "Will I be able to finish my work shift?"

"I don't see why not." The doctor opens his bag and pulls out a pair of gloves. He takes out some gauze and a bottle of rubbing alcohol. He starts cleaning the bus driver's arm. "But after this shift, may I suggest you take a couple of days offs."

The bus driver begins to feel the sting from the alcohol and closes his eyes tightly. "Ouch"

"I know it's a bit painful, but it has to be done. Please lower your hand so I can add some iodine to it."

The bus driver looks at the brown bottle and sees the doctor pouring the iodine on some cotton balls. "Is it going to hurt?"

"You might feel a sting and it is going to foam a bit, but do not worry." The doctor dabs his arm slightly avoiding any pressure. He then applies a layer of cotton dressing. "Now then, I am doing to have to bandage your arm tightly."

"Could someone please tell us what is going on?" Asked Thomas

The bus driver looks at Thomas. "I had a dispute with a loading passenger. I have to follow my route. I am not allowed to make any unnecessary stops."

Raymond looks inside the bus and sees shards of glass by some of the seats. "Is it safe to ride in?"

"It's perfectly safe. I assure you." said the bus driver "I just have to sweep it a little."

The doctor looks at Thomas and Raymond "Would any of you lend a hand and help sweep the bus?"

Astonished by the question Raymond shouts "How dare you ask such a ridiculous question."

The doctor frowns at them.

"The nerve of some people." Said Thomas

"It was only a suggestion." Said the doctor

"Doctor," said Raymond "We have an oath in this town."

"What oath?" asked the Doctor while adding tape around the bus driver's arm to hold the bandages secure.

The bus driver interrupts. "It's perfectly fine." He turns slightly and sees the broken glass scattered on the bus. "I will sweep up the glass afterward."

"What is the oath!" shouts the doctor in anger

"Do not inconvenience anybody!" said Mrs. Peterson and Mildred

He looks at both ladies. "What does that mean?" The doctor begins to pack his bag

"It means we keep to ourselves." said Thomas "We don't believe in getting involved in other people's affairs."

Astonished with the oath the doctor puts his hand in a fist. "So none of you would lift a finger to help this man?" asked the doctor angrily

"It's not in our best interests. His radical decision to fight a passenger has already made us late to work in the next town." Said Mrs. Peterson

Sarcastically Mildred waves her arms. "Plus you applying bandages on him, well it's just making the situation worse."

The doctor not believing what he is hearing nods his head in disbelief. "I have sworn an oath to help those in need." Slowly the doctor begins to raise his voice. 'What am I suppose to do let him bleed to death!"

"How much longer until you are finished with him doctor?" asked Thomas

"I can't believe you people. This man has lost a lot of blood. I need to make sure he will be stable before he can continue driving the bus."

"Doctor perhaps you didn't hear us. We are already running late to our jobs and you detaining him is making it worse." Said Mrs. Peterson

"Your jobs are not important. This man life is!" shouts the doctor

"Doctor it's alight, this is what I go through on a daily basis. I hear complaints all the time. Not just from these folks, but from other passengers I have to pick up."

The doctor in disbelief finishes securing the bus driver's arm.

"Can you hurry up, so the bus driver can let us board the bus?" said Raymond

Angrily and frustrated the doctor shouts "Can't you people wait a minute. I'm about done." The doctor grabs hold of the bus driver's arm and takes one last inspection. "Can you move your fingers?"

The bus driver extends his hand in the air and wiggles his fingers. "Yes doctor, I believe I can."

"Are you feeling any discomfort or pain?"

Again the bus driver moves his arm around in a circular motion.

"Can you move your wrist for me?"

Thomas rolls his eyes "Come on doctor we can't wait here all day."

The doctor sees the others waiting at the bus entrance. He notices some of them glaring at him. "Now then, we will pay no attention to them. Please try to move your wrist."

The bus driver moves his wrist in a circular motion and shouts in pain.

"On a scale from one through ten, ten being painful, how bad is your pain?"

The bus driver begins to hear the others complain. "Oh get on with it!" shouts Raymond

"We are extremely late! Said Mildred

"I should have listened to my husband and taken the day off. Then I would not be in this mess." Said Mrs. Peterson

"Well, I will be hearing from my supervisor about my tardiness." Said Thomas

They all begin to nod in agreement. Raymond beings pounding the bus door with his fist. The bus driver sighs. "I think I better let them board the bus."

"Your health is more important than them arriving late to work. You could have died with the amount of blood you lost."

"It's no use doctor, these people will be late and so will the people at my next few stops."

The bus driver jumps off from the platform and stretches out his legs a bit and sees Billy. "I'm so glad you stuck around a bit longer. This is actually the doctors stop."

Billy looks at the bus driver. "Why are you telling me this?"

"Please take him with you back to town."

The doctor looks at Billy briefly. "My good man I am a traveling physician and I am stopping at every town on my way up north." The bus driver walks to the right side of the bus and unlocks a bottom compartment "Doc, it's open"

The doctor looks at Billy and makes a slight hand jester. "Please wait."

Billy's eyes get big and with a greedy smile he asks "What is in it for me?"

The doctor thinks briefly. "If you wait for me I will give you a free check-up."

Disappointed with the offer Billy sighs "I suppose."

The doctor walks to the side of the bus and grabs his shoulder bag and suitcase.

"Thank you, doctor." Said the bus driver smiling "I don't know what I would have done without your help." The bus driver closes the compartment and the back door to the bus.

"Think nothing of it."

They hear a window opening. "This is unbelievable, how much longer are you two going to be chatting?' Shouts Raymond

"This man's life was in danger and all of you think it's a joke!" shouts the doctor "I assure you, you will not lose your jobs for being late!"

"Good luck in this town." Said the bus driver as he was boarding

"Thank you, I'm going to need it."

The doctor and Billy watch as the bus pulls away.

"Well doc, it's just you and me." Said Billy

The doctor walks to the trolley and places his belongings in the middle seat. "I wouldn't sit there," said Billy

"Why not?"

"Because once I start driving things have a tendency to fall out and I am not stopping this trolley."

"You don't want to be held accountable."

Billy shakes his head. "No, I just don't want to stop."

"Unbelievable!' the doctor says in disappointment. He grabs his suitcase and moves closer to the front of the trolley. He places his items close to him. Billy begins to drive recklessly and avoids any stops. The doctor grips his bags tightly. "I say, do you always drive this way?"

Billy ignoring the doctor, steps on the gas. The doctor with the other hand tries to hold his hat down. "Be careful doctor unlike the bus, this trolley has no windows."

The doctor frowns slightly. "What's your hurry?"

Billy makes a sharp turn and the doctor uses both hands to grip tightly both bags. Within minutes a slight breeze enters the trolley and the doctor loses his hat on another sharp turn. The doctor looks behind him and sees his hat rolling towards the side of the road. Billy has a big smile on his face. "I warned you."

"Yes, you did." Said the doctor angrily

The doctor stays quiet the rest of the way. Autumn is in the air and they pass many trees on the long winding road. The doctor tries to look at the scenery, but Billy is driving too fast. They arrive outside a gate entrance. Billy pulls up right next to it and brakes hard. "This is where you get off."

The doctor grabs his belonging and stands next to the trolley. 'Can you point me to the mayor's office?"

Billy laughs slightly. "Why would I do that?"

"I need to speak with him."

"No sir."

"I promise I won't mention your reckless driving."

Billy continues to laugh. "That doesn't bother me in the slightest. You can complain about my driving all you want."

"Then why won't you tell me?"

 "Because of the incident earlier. I'm in too much of a hurry. I have already wasted too much time." Billy steps on the gas and speeds away. The doctor watches Billy get further and further away.

'Well, I can't stand around here all day waiting for him to return. I guess I have no choice, but to find the mayor's office myself." The doctor begins to walk to town and sees a few houses and shopping centers. He sees another trolley. A few people walk by him and turn around to whisper to themselves. He sees an elderly lady walking towards him. "Madam, can you please tell me where the mayor's office is?"

She looks at him slightly without saying a word. "I'm beginning to think people in this town are rude. Never the less I must press forward."

The doctor makes his way towards the center of town and sees a beautiful water fountain in the middle. The fountain is a statue of a mermaid carved in stone. He looks at it and sees bright color stones embellish her tail. "How unusual, I am very tempted to stick my hand in the water." He runs his hand slightly by the rim of the water and walks away. He sees a street sweeper cleaning nearby. "Sir, I beg of you can you please tell me where the mayor's office is?" The street sweeper ignores him and continues working. Out of frustration, he shouts "Can nobody in this town help me?"

He takes a deep breath and presses forward. He continues walking and sees a couple with a baby stroller walking by. Just as he is about to ask them, they rush right past him without even giving a glance. "I'm beginning to wonder if I am invisible." He stops slightly and looks around. Noticing a separate building with a darker exterior he walks to it. It's a small building with a few pillars in front. Two large potted plants are on each side of the entrance. There is a glass mosaic outlining on a red door. "I wonder," Says the doctor to himself. Just as he's about to knock on the door it opens suddenly and a man steps out shouting. "Yes, mayor I will see to it. Don't worry" The man looks at the doctor and shouts" mayor are expecting someone?"

The mayor, a short round fellow wearing a gray suit walks towards the door. He looks slightly at the mirror by the door and sees the doctor standing outside. He whispers to the man. "Get rid of him." The man begins to close the door behind him. "Sorry sir, no visitors."

Quickly the doctor puts his leg out and stops the door from closing. "I'm sorry but I must speak to the mayor."

The man begins to use force to close the door and again says in a firm voice. "No visitors."

"This is matter of life and death."

Astonished the man let's go of the doorknob and stands in front of the door.
"Life and death you say."

"Yes, please let me speak to the mayor."

The mayor hearing the commotion yells "very well, let him enter."

"You heard the mayor."

The Doctor nods his head and walks right by the man and into the mayor's office. The mayor looks at the doctor nervously. "You better not be wasting my time." They hear the door slam shut tight.

"Mr. Mayor my name is."

Just before the Doctor could introduce himself the mayor interrupts."Now, just wait a minute. I'll ask the questions."

The Doctor astonished "well that is a little unorthodox, but if it will give me an audience with you." The mayor walks to his desk and sits. He opens a bottom desk drawer and pulls out a glass and a bottle of brandy. The doctor stands in front of the desk and gestures if he can sit.

The mayor looks at the doctor. "Well if you must take a seat then do so." The mayor begins to pour himself a shot of brandy. "I don't know who you are, but because of you, I am taking a shot of brandy to calm my nerves. What is the idea barging in here scaring me half to death?" Just as the doctor was about to speak the mayor interrupts him again. "I've been the mayor of this town for the past twenty years and in all my life I have never experienced an intrusion like this." The mayor drinks the first shot quickly and begins to pour himself another glass. He is very nervous and begins to tremble slightly. The doctor seeing this stands up from his chair and leans forward.

He sees a name plaque on the desk. "Mayor Kiva please let me speak." The mayor begins to pour another shot and the doctor quickly places his hand on the glass. The mayor lifts his eyes and looks at the doctor with anger
"How dare you put your hand on my glass. What gives you the right!!?"

The doctor moves his hand from the glass "Mayor Kiva your excessive drinking will only cloud your judgment."

"Who are you to stop me? Are you a government spy?"

The doctor opens his briefcase and pulls out a business card. He hands it to the mayor. "My business card will answer that question."
The mayor looks the card over. Dr. Vlad Cooper internal medicine "You're a Doctor." He asks surprised. He pulls out a handkerchief and begins to wipe the sweat off his brow. "What a relief. I thought you were a government official." The mayor begins to hand back the doctor's business card. "I'm sorry to inform you, but we have no need for a doctor in this town."

Surprised the doctor places his hand on the desk. "Do you already have a practicing physician in this town?"

"No, and like I said we have no use for one."

"Who do the citizens see when they are ill?"

 "Doctor Cooper we have a saying in this town." The mayor begins to pour more brandy into his glass. "Do not inconvenience anyone."

"Yes. I've heard it before, but the citizens need to be checked for any underlying illness."

"We have lived in this town for many years. Our ancestors began that tradition and ever since then, it's been our way of living. We have no use for Doctors here. It will be a waste of your time."

"Mayor, I think it should be my decision if I agree with you or not. As a doctor, I have sworn an oath to save lives and that's what I am here to do. At least give me a month to see if anyone needs me."

The mayor paces behind his desk slightly "you sound convincing, but where will you set up your office?"

"I don't need a big room, just a small office I can work in."

"Well I want to keep my eye on you, so you don't fool the residents here. I'm going to have you set up in the next building." The mayor opens his desk drawer and pulls out a key. "Now I am a busy man and I don't want any trouble from you or our agreement will be terminated. I will give you a month to see if anyone goes to your office for a medical check-up and just so we are clear you can not force anyone to see you and no advertising." The mayor looks over at the doctor and puts out his hand to shake on it. Doctor Cooper takes a deep breath and shakes the mayor's hand.

The doctor has a concerned smile "thank you mayor for this opportunity."
"Well, don't thank me yet, you only have a month." He hands the doctor the key. The doctor grips it in his palm and nods his head. He leaves the mayor's office with excitement and goes to the building next door. Doctor Cooper has a big smile on his face. He unlocks the door and turns on the light. He sees a desk in the middle of the room and a few chairs scattered around. The doctor walks to the back room and sees a long table in the corner. "This could work." He says to himself Doctor Cooper begins to organize the office and starts moving the furniture around. He opens his suitcase and takes out his medical licenses and hangs them on the wall. He walks to the door and opens it slightly to see if anyone is curious about the new business there. "Most people seem to be avoiding this area." Doctor Cooper goes inside and sits at his desk.

Mayor Kiva walks to the window in his office and peeks through the blind. "The residents here are unaware of an outside visitor." Mayor Kiva scratches his head slightly. "It's a shame" He sees a construction worker coming towards his office. Just as he's about to knock the mayor opens his door quickly. "Come in, come in quickly."

"Thank you, Mayor, why all the rush?"

"Oh, I just don't want to cause a scene and alert anyone nearby of your presence."

The construction worker nods his head. "Now tell me again what you needed me to repair."

"I want to make a room addition to my office."

"That's going to take me some time to complete."

"It is your civil duty to assist the town mayor and forget the oath for now."

"But I have other obligations and this is going out of my way."

"The duty to assist in town obligations is a priority. Everything else you have to do must wait." The construction worker frowns and takes a look at the calendar in the mayor's office. "When did you want me to begin?"

Smiling Mayor Kiva says in a low whisper "as soon as possible."

"I shall return tomorrow and we can discuss the details."

Mayor Kiva smiles with agreement and pours himself a glass of brandy.

Weeks go by and the Doctor doesn't seem to be getting any visitors. He paces back and forth in the office. "Looks like I am going to have to pack up and leave this town." He walks to the door and sees the construction worker carrying a bucket of paint inside the Mayor's office. The construction worker steps outside briefly and beings to move his shoulder in a circular motion.

"I have an ointment that can help with your pain?"

"Who said I felt any pain." The construction worker goes back inside the mayor's office and continues to work. He lays out a plastic tarp and opens the paint can.

The mayor walks to his office carrying a box of pasties. The doctor looks at the mayor. "Mayor Kiva I have noticed that since I have been here you have consumed nothing but sweets in the morning.

"Dr. Cooper," He says in a low whisper "I don't go around telling you how to live your life, so don't start telling me how to live mine. If I want to eat doughnuts in the morning, I will. I do not need you to tell me otherwise."

The doctor looks at the mayor and stands slightly in his path. "I am only trying to protect you. You can end up with heart disease and that can lead to serious consequences."

"As I said Doctor Cooper I don't need any advice." Mayor Kiva enters the building and sees the construction worker stirring the paint. "That guy has some nerve."

The painter begins to pour the paint into the tray. Mayor Kiva opens his desk drawer and beings to drink whiskey. "That know it all doctor. Who does he think he is talking to me that way?" The Mayor continues to complain in a low voice.

"Mayor Kiva I grabbed the wrong color of paint I'm going to have to go into the next town to get the right color."

The Mayor looks angrily at the construction worker. "That will put us behind schedule."

"If you want the color to match I have no choice but to go!"

"How long is it going to take you?'

"At least a couple of days."

 "Are you serious!" said Mayor Kiva "No! I need it done by today!" Out of anger, he smashes the glass cup on the floor.

"Be reasonable. That is impossible."

The doctor begins to hear a loud commotion and begins to pack his items. "Well, my time here is up. Maybe I'll have better luck in the next town. Christmas is in a couple of days and I have nothing to show for my experience here. I just hope the next town Mayor won't ask for references."

The mayor raises his voice and begins to shout. "You have to finish by today. I don't care if you stay here all night!"

The construction worker grabs his coat and begins to walk out of the office. "I am not listing to you. What you are asking for is impossible. I quit!"

 "You can't quit! I am firing you!" yells the Mayor

"You are crazy! It was a mistake making your office a priority. Because of you, I failed in decorating the town for the holidays."

"You can't blame me! You had all night to work on that!"

"You are unbelievable. When am I supposed to rest!"

Just as the mayor was about to say something he places his right hand on his chest and falls to the ground knocking over a Christmas tree. The construction worker sees this and gets closer to the Mayor. Mayor Kiva with the little strength in him says in a low voice "Doctor"

In a panic, the construction worker asks "what do you mean?'

"Next door," said Mayor Kiva before passing out

The construction worker shouts and runs next door. Doctor Cooper meets him and rushes to the mayor's aid. Doctor Cooper begins to check his vitals and tells the construction worker to step outside. People in town begin to gather outside the mayor's office. Day becomes night and the people begin to worry. The weather begins to change slightly and light snow begins to fall.

The mayor's wife rushes to the door and the construction worker holds her back. Hours seem like days and seconds like an eternity. A larger crowd begins to build and everyone there is preparing for the worst.

Doctor Cooper sits by mayor Kiva side. The mayor begins to open his eyes and awaken. The doctor takes a deep breath. "I thought I almost lost you."

The mayor looks at the doctor with sincerity. "What happened?" he asked as he tries to get up.

"Don't get up. You need to regain your strength. You gave me quite a scare. You had a slight stroke."

"A stroke, how is that possible?"

"We can discuss that another day. For now, I think it is best if I alert the citizens that you are awake." The mayor lifts his head slightly and sees the doctor going to the door. The construction worker, the mayor's wife, and many others begin to enter the office. "All I ask of you all is do not overwhelm the mayor."

The mayor's wife gets close to her husband and has tears running down her face. "I thought I was going to lose you." She said

"You almost did my dear." The Mayor looks towards the doctor and sees him grabbing his suitcase and begins to head out. The Mayor calls out to him. "Doctor, where are you going?"

The doctor turns to look at the mayor. "My time here is up. I failed at my practice and I must move on."

Mayor Kiva begins to shout "Doctor, you can't leave. This town needs you. I need you."

"I'm afraid I don't understand."

The Mayor sits up slightly and shouts. Everyone listen to me. This here is the finest Doctor I know and if any of you feel pain please feel free to visit the doctor in his permanent location next door."

Doctor Cooper looks at the Mayor with tears of joy. "I don't know what to say."

"You have given me the greatest Christmas gift of all. You gave me another chance at life. I promise you this town will change. No longer will our motto be, do not inconvenience anybody, but instead the opposite."

The townspeople gather around Doctor Cooper and cheer with joy shouting Merry Christmas.

Wendy Doherty

Wendy Doherty is a contributing writer from Portage, Michigan. Her writing has been featured in *Breast Cancer Wellness Magazine*, *Faces of Inspiration – Breast Cancer Stories*, and *((Ring Ring)) Hello? Grandma's House. Big Bad Wolf Speaking.: A Christmas Anthology Part One.*

Wendy is a wife of 47 years, an advocate, breast cancer survivor, and a writer. She is currently working on her first novel.

Candied Fruit – Do Not Open!

By Wendy Doherty

It was 1964, and I was ten years old. The Christmas season was upon us. One day while my mother was out shopping, I got an intense craving for something sweet. After an exhaustive search, there was nothing to be found in the kitchen, in the usual places.

In desperation, I decided to check my mother's cupboard which housed the baking supplies. I found a container of candied fruit. I did not know why we had this food or what its intended purpose was. It never occurred to me that I should ask.

I opened the sealed container and helped myself to a modest sample. I knew not to eat too many. Without having measured, I assume I helped myself to one Tablespoon's worth of the candied fruit. I was not impressed with its taste. Thinking no one would notice and in an effort to disguise my offense, I spread the candied fruit around and resealed the container. I put it back in the cupboard and had forgotten about the candied fruit until…

The following weekend my mother bellowed out my name. "W e n d y!" I could tell by her tone she was irritated. Her words to me were, "I see you helped yourself to the candied fruit. I was planning on using it in a recipe for Christmas dinner." All I could think of to say was, "Well, they were in the cupboard." As if to imply they were fair game and that this wasn't such a big deal. I offered to pay my mother for the fruit, thinking this would make amends, but she refused and yelled, "I don't want your money!"

One or two days before Christmas, my mother followed me into the kitchen. She reached up and grabbed the container of candied fruit. She opened her recipe book, stared, and sighed. Then she slammed the book shut and said, "No! I'm not going to make it." I said nothing and watched her storm out of the kitchen. I thought she was being a tad dramatic.

Christmas Day arrived and I thought all was well. After dinner, we were sitting in the living room and talking. I thought it was unusual that my grandmother was sitting so close to my mother. It was as if they presented a unified front.

The adults were commenting on how good Christmas Dinner was. That in itself was noteworthy. My family was not eager to participate in after-dinner-conversation. Without warning, my mother uttered unkind and hurtful words. "Well, we would have had a nicer dessert, but Wendy helped herself to the candied fruit!" My father looked at me and glared. I stared back at him.

Wait a minute! We just had three desserts! All I ate was one Tablespoon of the not-so-tasty candied fruit. The container remained nearly full. I shrugged it off, thinking the topic was dead. I did not appreciate being shamed in front of everyone.

During Christmas vacation, my grandmother invited me to spend the night. Of course, I said, "Yes." While we were talking, Grandma mentioned the candied fruit incident. She said, "Do you understand what Mama was saying?" I decided this would be a good time to play dumb and I told her "No." Grandma went on to say, "Mama was counting on this ingredient for a recipe for Christmas. Because you helped yourself, Mama didn't have enough to make the dessert she wanted." Hmm. *I was thinking there was plenty left. What was it with the stupid dried candied fruit?!* How did it go from being an infraction to an international incident? I responded with, "Oh." *And since when, did my Grandmother refer to my mom as Mama?*

I thought this was the end of the transgression and shame, however, I was wrong.

About two months later, I was in the kitchen making myself lunch or a snack. My mother followed me to the kitchen. She reached up into the cupboard and grabbed the container of candied fruit.

She stretched out her arm and in a negative tone said: "Here, you might as well have this. You've already helped yourself." What?! That was it! In an annoyed tone of voice, I said: "I don't want it!" There was no way I was going to accept the candied fruit after all the shame and blame that had been bestowed upon me.

My mother's terse reply was: "Well, what am I going to do with it?" I suggested she throw it out and I walked away.

Perhaps I missed an important life lesson. At the time, it seemed like much ado about nothing. The following year during the Christmas season, I was warned not to open any food without permission. In retrospect, it seems my mother could have told all three of her children which food items were forbidden fruit and off-limits.

After 58 years, the only thing I have to say is, "Forgive me, Mother. For I have sinned." Had I been on my toes, in 1974, I could have offered my firstborn as an act of penitence.
To this day, I have never looked at another package of candied fruit, and never will.

 The holidays were stressful in my childhood home. This was largely due to my father's alcoholism. We had to walk on eggshells and be prepared for anything. It was exhausting. This particular year, I thought Christmas was going to come and go without a stressor. I was wrong. In the overall scheme of life, this was not a catastrophe. Did the situation merit discipline? Probably. It did not warrant embarrassment, blaming, and shaming on the most important holiday of the year.

My advice to parents: Let your children be children. They will make mistakes. Some are big ones and others not-so-much. Let it be and let it go.

"I set a personal record on Christmas. I got my shopping done three weeks ahead of time. I had all the presents back at my apartment, I was halfway through wrapping them, and I realized, 'Damn, I used the wrong wrapping paper.' The paper I used said, 'Happy Birthday.' I didn't want to waste it,
so I just wrote 'Jesus' on it."

– Demetri Martin

"The outdoor Christmas lights, green and red and gold and blue and twinkling, remind me that most people are that way all year round — kind, generous, friendly and with an occasional moment of ecstasy. But Christmas is the only time they dare reveal themselves."

– Harlan Miller

Kristina Hutchinson

Kristina Hutchinson lives in Dunbar, West Virginia with her family. She enjoys crocheting, reading, and watching vintage soap operas. She is currently working on her second novel, a coming of age story set in WW2 England.

Kristina Hutchinson lives in Dunbar, West Virginia with her family. She enjoys crocheting, reading, and watching vintage soap operas. She is currently working on her second novel, a coming of age story set in WW2 England.

Fascination

By Kristina Hutchinson

Jessamyn Coulier had never told a lie, not even a little white lie. Until now. As she stood behind the counter of Bentley's bookstore she composed herself before speaking to her best friend and boss Janine Bentley.

"Janine, I need an aspirin."

"What's wrong?" her boss stopped what she was doing and looked at her employee with concern.

"I feel a headache coming on I don't think I'll be able to go to the party tonight-"

"But Jess it's Christmas Eve and everyone will be there."

"Yes, but I'll be the only one without a date." Jess reasoned. She began to fidget with the bow on her blouse.

"So that's it,' Janine mused. "You don't have a headache after all."

"Maybe not, but I guarantee I will tonight when everyone asks why I'm still single."

"You know you could look at it as an opportunity to meet someone new." Her boss offered.

"I'm afraid I won't be that lucky. " Jess sat down behind the counter and picked up the latest paperback holiday romance she'd been reading.

"Love isn't about luck., Jess." Janine sighed.

"But look what you and Trace have." Janine and her husband had met in high school but had been seeing other people. Then in college, they were fixed up on a blind date by his sister. And they are living happily ever after. "It's magical."

"Love isn't magic either. Yes, there was a spark between Trace and me when we first met and I swear I even heard bells, but it took years of being with the wrong people and then a blind date to finally get together. It's been a lot of work.' the bell over the front door jingled. ".Mrs. Atkins is coming ."

Jess set her book aside and waited on the older woman, "I have your order ready, Mrs. Atkins. The books came yesterday. ' she reached under the counter and brought out a small stack of hardcovers. "Would you like them wrapped?"

"Oh yes, dear. Thank you. You're both such sweet girls. Do you have anything special planned for tonight?"

"No-" Jess started to say.

"We're going to Cyrus later for drinks." Janine cut in.

"Sounds like fun.' the customer smiled warmly. " How much do I owe you?"....

And that is how the rest of the day went. The constant jingle of the bell over the door as familiar faces came and went. Shoppers looking for the perfect last-minute gift.

Jess had to admit they had a good thing going at the shoppe in the heart of beautiful downtown Waterbury, Massachusetts. Upstairs was the dance studio where she taught part-time and her apartment.

At a quarter till six, Janine came out of her office. "Where are the keys?' she asked. " I think we should lock up. It'll give us time to get ready to go to the bar."

"You go without me. I hate to be a Debbie Downer…"

"I'm not leaving you alone on Christmas eve." Her boss and best friend told her flatly.

The bell above the door jingled again and this time a young man walked in wearing dark blue jeans and a suede jacket. He took off his hat revealing rich waves of chestnut hair. He dusted the snow off the shoulders of his jacket. Janine's eyes just about popped as she and Jess exchanged glances. With chocolate brown eyes and a chiseled jawline, he was definitely eye candy.

"May I help you with something?" Jess spoke up.

"I'd like to browse. If that's alright." The young guy smiled.

"Just browsing? That's what they all do five minutes till closing." Janine let out a sigh.

"Janine, let him look around. Sir, let me know if you need any assistance."

"Thanks. I will." and he disappeared among the rows of bookshelves.

"Not bad looking eh?" Janine raised an eyebrow.

"Shh."

***

Jess sat down behind the counter and went through a list of online orders while Janine went into the back.

Tap. Tap.

Jess looked up. It was a soft tapping. Probably just the snow falling upon the roof.

Tap tap.

"There it is again." She set her laptop aside and got up from behind the counter.

She followed the sound as it got louder. Tap tap. It was coming from the hobby section. When she rounded the shelves she saw the stranger tapping his feet on the hardwood floor. Was he dancing? Jess let out a giggle and the young man dropped the book he had been holding. Jess picked it up and read the cover. *WALTZING FOR BEGINNERS*.

"Excuse me Sir, but are you trying to waltz?"

The stranger shrugged shyly. "I'm doing it all wrong aren't I?"

"Yes, but it's not entirely your fault. You can't learn to dance from a book. And to learn the waltz you need a partner."

"Then I'm in trouble. I need to learn how to dance for my sister's wedding on Saturday."

"This Saturday?' she asked. He nodded. "That's cutting it close. Well, show me what moves you have."

He literally did the 'running man' in the HOBBY section. Jess almost choked as she tried to keep herself from laughing out loud. She hadn't seen dance moves that bad since high school. "You definitely could use a lesson. Listen, we're closing soon, but I think I can help you." Jess went to the front door and flipped the sign to "CLOSED". She turned to the young man. "If you're serious about learning the waltz then we have to do it properly."

"How?"

They were now standing close, facing one another. Jess couldn't believe how soft his brown eyes were. She had a weakness for chocolate brown eyes. Enough. She told herself. Focus. "We start with the basic steps.' she continued. ' Face me. Why are you laughing?"

"I'm a bit nervous. I haven't danced with anyone since prom." He confessed.

"Really? Did you do the 'running man' at prom?"

He nodded, his cheeks reddening.

"Wow, your poor date.' She put her hands on his shoulders. 'Don't be nervous, the waltz is easy to learn, just follow me. As the leader, your right-hand goes on the small of my back. A good rule is to never pull or push, but rather lead with the body, not the arm. Got it?"

"I think so." The stranger followed her directions and Jess felt a rush of electricity at his gentle touch. Focus, she reminded herself.

"Now, step forward with your left foot. I step back with my right. You step back with your right foot. I step forward with my left foot. Very good... Those are the basic steps."

"Is that it? It's easier than it looked in the book."

"As I said before you can't learn to dance from a book. Now that you learned how to box step, you need to learn how to travel around the room since the Waltz is a traveling dance."

"I'm a travel agent so it should be easy." He smiled.

"Be serious now." She told him, but she couldn't help but smile, too. They moved around the room and Jess showed him the key to making the waltz look better was the rise and fall. He caught on quickly. " Now let's try it with music." She took out her phone and scrolled through a playlist. The 'Christmas Waltz' seemed appropriate.

The bookstore was soon filled with the soothing sound of violins.

"That's pretty. Is that Frank Sinatra singing?" He asked.

"Yep. That's Ol' Blue Eyes. You like Sinatra?"

"Doesn't everyone? He was such an amazing singer and actor." He stepped forward and she stepped back.

"You've seen his movies?"

"I've watched a few Rat Pack films.' he told her. " My mother is a big fan. Sammy Davis, Jr is her favorite."

"Mine too. Are you spending Christmas with your mom?"

He nodded. "The whole family. We have a cabin north of here and we're getting together to go skiing before the wedding."

"That's this weekend. A December wedding sounds romantic." Was Jess blushing now?

"Are you going to spend Christmas with your family as well?" He asked, his own face becoming warm.

 "My family lives out of state' she explained. ' But Janine, she owns this store, she's my best friend and we've been invited out. "

"That's great. No one should be alone this time of year.' The young man's eyes glinted as he added thoughtfully: "You know what this song reminds me of...the old carousel that used to be here downtown."

"I remember that too!"

"Every year, right?'

"And on the corner was Glenn's Department store," Jess added the memories of her childhood came flooding back.

"They went out of business when the Mall was built."

"Downtown hasn't been the same without it." she shook her head.

"You feel that way, too?"

Jess nodded. "Remember the stand outside the store, selling chestnuts?"

"Yea. His name was Rayburn and his wife sold bags of scented pinecones."

"They smelled of cinnamon."

"Great memories." The stranger agreed.

" The best."

"Can I turn you?" He asked with newfound confidence.

Jess nodded and they turned around each other clockwise.

"You're getting good at this" She enthused.

"I have a great teacher. Where did you learn to dance so well? You must have taken lessons."

"When I was four, Papa started me out in ballet then later tap dancing. Now I teach a class on Wednesdays in my studio upstairs, you're welcome to join us one night."

"I'm only in town for the wedding. I live in Salem."

"Oh," she tried to hide the disappointment in her voice. She decided to change the subject. "You said you were a travel agent? I bet that's exciting."

"It can be. But I'm behind a desk much of the time. The part I enjoy the most is being able to make people's dreams come true."

He turned her again. So smoothly. So effortlessly. Jess might have been a good teacher, but the way he moved with such easy grace, he was the perfect partner. Was this really the same guy who only moments ago had been so awkward?

The music ended.

There was the sound of someone clapping.

The dancers stopped suddenly and Jess realized they were still in the bookstore and not some castle in the air. "Janine, you're here?"

"I've been here."

Before her dance partner left, Jess made a bold move and gave him her card. 'In case you're in town again and want another dance lesson.'

The handsome stranger took a chance as well and gave her his card. ' In case you want a dance partner.'

***

"A nice guy.' Janine said thoughtfully as she locked up. "That was a good thing you did."

"He's pretty nice." Jess confided.

"You like him." It was more of a statement than a question.

Jess nodded.

"Do you think he'll be back?"

"He said he's only in town for a short time," Jess explained as she pulled on her parka.

"Then you probably won't ever see him again?"

"I don't know.' She shrugged, before adding: "But maybe that's part of the magic. "

And yes, Jess still believed in the magic especially now after meeting this stranger, but Janine had been right: real magic doesn't work alone. Jess opened her hand and looked at the card it held. Darren Fremont Travel Agent.

Janine turned the lights off and the two stepped out into the falling snow. She looked at her friend and raised an eyebrow: 'To Cyrus'?"

Jess shrugged. "Why not."

Maybe things were finally going Jessamyn Coulier's way, after all, Salem wasn't that far. And a phone number was a good start!

Bob Slivatz

Bob graduated from St. James High School in Ferndale and joined the Army where he served with the 82nd Airborne Division, the 6th and 1st Special Forces Group. Upon returning from overseas he attended Wayne State University and joined the Detroit Police Department where he retired from the 7th Precinct. He also worked as a plaster/drywall repairman with "M.S. Plastering Company," and as a commercial diver for "Sea Side Diving Inc., St Clair Shores."

A published editorialist since 1976, he has written three books: "From Inside Now Out," "True Tales from an Enigmatic Mind," and "Poems from an Enigmatic Mind," as well as being a contributing author for "Christmas Anthology Part One." He is also a columnist for "The Drop" the Special Forces (The Green Berets) Association magazine; columnist for "The Paraglide" the 82nd Airborne Division Association, and past contributing columnist for "The Beacon NewsMagazine."

He also plays the guitar and formerly played with "The Nealson Rating," "BANDit," and currently "Just Jammin." Married to his wife Lynn for 46 years he is a pet lover and currently owns three cats residing in Richmond, MI.

The Bulge

By Bob Slivatz

"The Bulge" was the name given to one of the bloodiest battles of WWII when the Germans tried everything to break through the allied army lines and cut their supply routes, choke them off, and destroy them that went from December 16th, 1944 through January 25th, 1945.

It came as a surprise attack against the allied forces who were quickly overtaken, overwhelmed, and broken.

It was the first time the 82nd and 101st Airborne Divisions had ever been trucked into battle rather than coming in by parachute or glider. They were going to "plug the hole" in the allied lines and drive the Germans back. A poster was later made with a soldier walking and saying "I'm the 82nd Airborne and this is as far as the bastards are going." The 82nd was no stranger to combat. They were the best America had through North Africa, Sicily, Italy, Normandy, Holland and now they were going up against the best the Germans had to offer. T was a good start!

"The Bulge" was the name given to one of the bloodiest battles of WWII when the Germans tried everything to break through the allied army lines and cut their supply routes, choke them off, and destroy them that went from December 16th, 1944 through January 25th, 1945.

It came as a surprise attack against the allied forces who were quickly overtaken, overwhelmed, and broken.

It was the first time the 82nd and 101st Airborne Divisions had ever been trucked into battle rather than coming in by parachute or glider. They were going to "plug the hole" in the allied lines and drive the Germans back. A poster was later made with a soldier walking and saying "I'm the 82nd Airborne and this is as far as the bastards are going." The 82nd was no stranger to combat. They were the best America had through North Africa, Sicily, Italy, Normandy, Holland and now they were going up against the best the Germans had to offer. The airborne has only one saying "All The Way" as they'd never lost an inch of ground in combat and they weren't about to start now.

Albert was assigned as the acting first sergeant of Batter B, 80th Anti Aircraft (Anti Tank) Battalion of the 82nd Airborne who was part of the glidermen cited by General James Gavin for saving the Drop Zone in Niejmegan, Holland during "Operation Market Garden" (better known as "A Bridge Too Far."). The airborne units had fought for weeks in Holland and were reequipping and regrouping after a costly bloody campaign and here they were again, thrown into the thick of battle without winter gear being issued or complete supplies to face the best of the German army once again except this time in trucks.

The 101st Airborne was to take and hold the town of Bastogne, the major crossroads for approaching German tanks. The 82nd was to drive further ahead, stop, push back, and destroy the Germans at all costs.

The fighting was fierce, sometimes hand to hand, yet the 82nd airborne not only stopped the Germans but were destroying them on the battlefield and pushing them back. Every day it was moving forward, attack, attack, attack.

Albert had the flu which was draining him. He was exhausted after the Holland campaign and they never had time for proper rest and recovery before they were again thrown into the heart of darkness, and the best the Germans had to offer. They had been fighting for weeks, only to dig another fox hole for a remain overnight position ("RON") and move out again the next day. A Brit was good enough to come by and bring Albert a canteen full of hot tea with brandy. Battery B's job was to search out and destroy the enemy.

As night fell it got bitter cold. The clouds began breaking and at times they could see the stars which made it seem colder. They could hear and feel intermittent artillery from both sides. Their ears strained against the night darkness to hear any sign of an approaching enemy.

Was that a twig snapping from the weight of the snow? Snow falling off a branch in the slight breeze? A German scout probing the lines looking for soft spots or trying to kill those they came across asleep in the foxholes?

A slight fog was hanging over the ground making visibility even worse. One could barely see five feet in front of themselves. Albert was using all his senses to detect any threat approaching. Using his field glasses straining his eyes for any break in the fog outline of anybody or anything as his duties were to always make sure his men came out of battle alive. Nothing was going to get by him. He was carrying a Browning Automatic Rifle

(BAR) which could lay down an impressive six hundred and fifty rounds a minute fed by a twenty round box magazine. The most formidable weapon Albert had carried throughout the war.

Strain as he did, he couldn't see anything through the fog. He fought to stay awake as the cold, combat and fatigue tore at every fiber of his body. War was Hell is the old saying and nothing could be further closer to reality. Men dying or wounded crying out for their mothers, their wives, girlfriends, or just writhing in pain as their bodies were torn to shreds by guns, knives, bombs, bullets, and grenades, to say nothing of the freezing cold in the winter and the heat and humidity during the summer. The sleepless nights, the constant tension or war, the short and cold rations carried and eaten when one could as "normal" hours did not apply. Ones' goal was to simply take it one day at a time and to try to live through that day and keep your buddies alive while destroying the enemy. In battle the Airborne motto was "All The Way" and they had proven themselves time and time again.

Strain through he could, Albert felt frustrated by the fatigue and the fog blocking his vision. Pitch dark was bad enough, but a ground fog could let the enemy sneak up without you knowing it. The Germans were very good at this technique and used it to strike fear into their enemies. Here the allies were up against the very best Germany had to offer who were intent on breaking the allied lines and driving them from fortress Europe.

Feeling what he thought was a German infiltrator entering his foxhole and attempting to grab him by the back of his neck, Albert took out his bayonet and stabbed, stabbed, stabbed, stabbed, intent on killing his attacker.

"Sarge! Sarge! Sarge! It's OK! IT'S OK!" Albert suddenly became aware of a voice above him. The voice sounded familiar but all around seemed confusing. He was being shaken and he knew he had his bayonet in his hand.

"Sarge! Sarge! It's me, Dixon. It's okay. You must have fallen asleep. You're fine."

Albert finally came to his full senses and acknowledged Dixon on top of him.

"You must have hit the zone, Sarge, as you sure killed the hell out of your binocular straps, that's for sure. Good thing it wasn't a German as there wouldn't have been enough to identify the way you were going" said Dixon with a bit of wry humor to lighten the situation.

"Thanks, Dixon!" said Albert. "It's a good thing you caught me before I hurt any of our men. I don't know what it was but I thought for sure a Kraut was crawling in my foxhole."

"Twilight sleep Sarge," said Dixon. "They can't expect us to stay awake and fight forever with no rest and little in the way of chow. But it's the Army, what do you expect?! You going to be alright now?!"

"Yeah, you can bet your life on it," said Albert.

The airborne has only one saying "All The Way" as they'd never lost an inch of ground in combat and they weren't about to start now.

Albert was assigned as the acting first sergeant of Batter B, 80th Anti Aircraft (Anti Tank) Battalion of the 82nd Airborne who was part of the glidermen cited by General James Gavin for saving the Drop Zone in Niejmegan, Holland during "Operation Market Garden" (better known as "A Bridge Too Far."). The airborne units had fought for weeks in Holland and were reequipping and regrouping after a costly bloody campaign and here they were again, thrown into the thick of battle without winter gear being issued or complete supplies to face the best of the German army once again except this time in trucks.

The 101st Airborne was to take and hold the town of Bastogne, the major crossroads for approaching German tanks. The 82nd was to drive further ahead, stop, push back, and destroy the Germans at all costs.

The fighting was fierce, sometimes hand to hand, yet the 82nd airborne not only stopped the Germans but were destroying them on the battlefield and pushing them back. Every day it was move forward, attack, attack, attack.

Strain as he did, he couldn't see anything through the fog. He fought to stay awake as the cold, combat and fatigue tore at every fiber of his body. War was Hell is the old saying and nothing could be further closer to reality. Men dying or wounded crying out for their mothers, their wives, girlfriends, or just writhing in pain as their bodies were torn to shreds by guns, knives, bombs, bullets, and grenades, to say nothing of the freezing cold in the winter and the heat and humidity during the summer. The sleepless nights, the constant tension or war, the short and cold rations carried and eaten when one could as "normal" hours did not apply. Ones' goal was to simply take it one day at a time and to try to live through that day and keep your buddies alive while destroying the enemy. In battle the Airborne motto was "All The Way" and they had proven themselves time and time again.

Strain through he could, Albert felt frustrated by the fatigue and the fog blocking his vision. Pitch dark was bad enough, but a ground fog could let the enemy sneak up without you knowing it. The Germans were very good at this technique and used it to strike fear into their enemies. Here the allies were up against the very best Germany had to offer who were intent on breaking the allied lines and driving them from fortress Europe.

Feeling what he thought was a German infiltrator entering his foxhole and attempting to grab him by the back of his neck, Albert took out his bayonet and stabbed, stabbed, stabbed, stabbed, intent on killing his attacker.

"Sarge! Sarge! Sarge! It's OK! IT'S OK!" Albert suddenly became aware of a voice above him. The voice sounded familiar but all around seemed confusing. He was being shaken and he knew he had his bayonet in his hand.

"Sarge! Sarge! It's me, Dixon. It's okay. You must have fallen asleep. You're fine."

Albert finally came to his full senses and acknowledged Dixon on top of him.

"You must have hit the zone, Sarge, as you sure killed the hell out of your binocular straps, that's for sure. Good thing it wasn't a German as there wouldn't have been enough to identify the way you were going" said Dixon with a bit of wry humor to lighten the situation.

"Thanks, Dixon!" said Albert. "It's a good thing you caught me before I hurt any of our men. I don't know what it was but I thought for sure a Kraut was crawling in my foxhole."

"Twilight sleep Sarge," said Dixon. "They can't expect us to stay awake and fight forever with no rest and little in the way of chow. But it's the Army, what do you expect?! You going to be alright now?!"

"Yeah, you can bet your life on it," said Albert.

He stayed awake through the rest of the night and pure adrenaline. Watching, listening, waiting for any sign of the enemy. There was a war to fight.

As dawn rose, Albert felt better. They could hear sporadic artillery and hear planes overhead but had no idea if it was ours or theirs. Going from foxhole to foxhole he checked on his men to see if they had all made it safely through the night.

He was met by a runner while doing his rounds.

"First Sergeant, Captain Cliff said for you guys to get ready to go on the move again. No hot chow with turkey and gravy this day" said the runner.

"Hot chow with turkey and gravy?" asked the first sergeant in a bit of dismay.

"Yeah Sarge, the Captain also said to wish you a Merry Christmas!"

"Christmas?!?!?!?"

"Yeah Sarge, today is December 25th, it's officially Christmas!"

Albert finished making the rounds of his men wishing them all a Merry Christmas and telling them he's gotten the word that they would soon be on the move.

"Hey Top!" asked one of the other glidermen. "Think we'll make it to New Year?!"

"Damn straight we are! We're going to kick these Krauts all the way back to Berlin until they surrender unconditionally and we're all going home together. Nothing can stop us from our mission to go 'All The Way!!'"

"Once again we find ourselves enmeshed in the Holiday Season, that very special time of year when we join with our loved ones in sharing centuries-old traditions such as trying to find a parking space at the mall. We traditionally do this in my family by driving around the parking lot until we see a shopper emerge from the mall, then we follow her, in very much the same spirit as the Three Wise Men, who 2,000 years ago followed a star, week after week, until it led them to a parking space."

– Dave Berry

C J Lawson

C J Lawson was born in St. Petersburg Florida. His family moved to Michigan when he was 6, and it was his Junior High school years that introduced him to the exciting, creative world of Fiction writing.

Through Junior, as well as High school, he was approached more than once to enter his work in Young Authors Contests but never chose to take his writing to the next level. His first novel – IS, was published in 2017. He is currently working on the sequel to his SciFi/thriller, titled – IS TOO (The Other).

The Christmas Coin

By C.J.Lawson

Just as the sun was setting in the late December sky, 8-year-old Robbie Baron sat on the edge of his bed, nose pressed against the cold glass window, amidst the partially unpacked cardboard boxes that engulfed his new room. It was still snowing outside. He could keep track of how much had fallen from the drift that covered an old picnic table in the back yard. If this was his old house, he would be out there in it. He and his best friends, Todd and Mike. They loved making snow forts and taking their sleds down the steep embankment behind their school, only a block away. But this wasn't his old house. And his best friends in the whole world were now gone.

This would be the worst Christmas ever. In fact, he felt as though his life was ruined. He and his parents made the move less than a week ago, leaving behind his friends, and everything normal…and good. How could they do this to him? How could they expect him to carry on in this foreign new place? And even worse yet, after Christmas break, he would be walking into a new school. That's it… his life was over. "Hope you like your new job," he mumbled, teary-eyed, as his breath left behind a moist patch on the glass, and he drew a frown center of it.

Seconds later, his door opened and he could immediately see the reflection of his Mother's silhouette standing there - the bright hallway behind her. "Hey, you want to help me bake some cookies?" she asked

I'll pass" he said, not even bothering to turn around "Oh come on Robbie, we always bake cookies together at Christmas time."

"Yeah, when I was 6," he responded.

"Honey, I know you're mad, but your friends –

"Best friends," he interrupted. She paused, took in a deep breath, and quickly let it out.

"Are only an hour away. I told you, we can go visit the old neighborhood anytime you want to."

"It's not the same, Mom!" he snapped.

"Honey, don't you think you'll make some new friends?"

"I had friends. I don't want any new ones," he answered, finally turning his head so she could see the disappointment on his face.

"Ok. I'll be in the kitchen if you change your mind," she said, closing his door.

After his mother left, he could hear the music from 'A Charley Brown Christmas' coming from the living room, just like every Christmas before. They know that's my favorite, he thought. "Nice try guys," he blurted out. It wasn't the same. He felt it was all so fake…and stupid. After all, he wasn't sure he even believed in Santa, anymore. How could things get any worse? He turned to kick a box when out the corner of his eye, he saw movement in his window. It must have been a bird, or perhaps a squirrel. He hopped up on his bed and looked outside. The snow was falling lighter now and seemed as though it might soon stop.

To his amazement, the small drift that sat on the ledge outside his window appeared to be untouched. No sign that any animal had been there at all. It was getting even darker outside by now, but without turning on his bedroom light, he went to one of the cardboard boxes and returned with a flashlight. Next, he aimed the bright beam out into the yard, where he saw what looked to be small prints in the snow that went from below his window, and across the yard as far as he could see. "Whatever," he said, acting as if nothing had made him curious, or even just a tad bit nervous. But, when the time came for Robbie to go to bed that night, he would be found with that same flashlight clutched tightly in both hands.

The next morning, Robbie awoke to the smell of bacon, and once again, the sound of Christmas music ringing throughout the house. He quickly stood up on his bed and looked out the window. The tracks were gone. Maybe he didn't really see any tracks at all? Or maybe it snowed again after he went to sleep, covering them over? He made his way to the kitchen.

"Hey, did it snow any more last night after I went to bed?" he asked.

"Good morning to you too," his mother said.

"Nope," answered his Dad.

"Are you sure?"

"Yup, cleared the snow off the cars last night, and when we got up this morning, everything looked the same." Robbie could feel a tinge of excitement run down his back. And as his Mother served him up some breakfast, he felt he couldn't get outside, and on to his new mystery, quick enough. Finally, something to be excited about.

As he traveled out into the yard, the crunch under his boots told him it was good packing snow.   Good for making snowmen, or forts. Only, he had something far more interesting to deal with. There were no tracks anywhere. But he continued across the yard in the direction he saw or at least thought he saw, the tracks leading. Once he got to the far end of the yard, he was ready to write the whole thing off and return inside, when he noticed the morning sun reflecting off of something half-buried in the snow at his feet. But it wasn't until he bent down, that he could see it was a coin. He lifted it from the snow and inspected it. It was small, and it looked to be made of silver. At first, he thought it was a dime. But he had never seen anything like this before. It appeared very old, and with crazy markings on it. Old, but new. As if it had been polished. Tilting it a bit, the sun reflected a blinding glimmer. He looked around to see if anyone was watching, and quickly stuffed it in the right front pocket of his jeans.

"Robbie, time to go shopping!" his mother shouted.

"Be right there!" he yelled back. Finally giving in to his curiosity, Robbie scanned the yard one last time, and then to his bedroom window. A few seconds later, he headed back into the house.

That night, he laid there in bed with his flashlight, exploring everything about his new find. One side had three stars with strange writing, and the other side had what appeared to be a moon with half a moon beside it. The mystery of it all had his imagination running wild. So he laid there, imagining a number of thrilling possibilities, and all the while rubbing the coin between his thumb and forefinger with his right hand, still clutching the flashlight tightly with his left until his eyelids became too heavy to stay awake any longer.

In a dream, his mind took him on a magical ride. He was flying over beautiful snow-covered landscapes and ice-covered lakes. Over tall city buildings with streets lined in brightly covered Christmas lights. Making his way over drift covered roofs, and quiet neighborhood roads, when -

"Robbie." A strange and soft voice filled his head.

"What?" he responded, still within his magical journey.

"I am Bonki, and it is necessary that I speak with you. I'm going to bring you out of your dream now, and there is no reason to be afraid."

And Robbie wasn't afraid. He felt strange, but also comfortable. It was as if he were in the presence of an old friend. Slowly, his magnificent picture started to fade, until Robbie found himself staring at his bedroom door. The moonlight that poured through his window behind him also presented the shadow of someone or something within it on the wall in front of him.

Robbie laid there still, holding his breath, hoping to awaken from what he could only imagine was still a dream. He finally took a breath and blinked hard twice. It was still there. He then made up his mind that he would turn quickly, and face whatever was there...if anything. He would count to 5. He got to 3 when there were suddenly 3 taps on the glass. "Game on," he whispered when he quickly spun around and saw him. Robbie dropped his flashlight and it came on after hitting the floor, illuminating the back half of his room, and his new guest. The thought of what could be was so much more frightening than what he actually found there...staring at him from the other side of the window. He wasn't frightening at all. Robbie felt a warm comforting feeling wash over him, and a smile slowly began to lift his cheeks. He couldn't help it. He felt happy.

He was very small, but with a young man's face. His hair was blond and curly and hung just below his ears. His skin was very fair, and his nose and cheeks were kind of red. His eyes appeared bright blue, and atop his blonde curls sat an old green silk looking cap. He just kept smiling at Robbie, as if he had no other expression. Robbie hopped to his feet and slid open his window.
"Hello, Robbie," he finally said. And it was then that Robbie got a closer view of his guest. He appeared to have a matching green silk jacket, and Robbie was overwhelmed by the smell of cotton candy. Also, for being a small man of maybe 3 feet in height, Robbie was curious as to how he was able to remain in the window, which had to be 6 feet from the ground. Robbie didn't bother to ask; wasn't sure he knew how.

"Hello? Who are you?" Robbie asked.

"As I said before, I'm Bonki."

"Bonki - like in my dream," Robbie replied.

"No, Bonki - exactly from your dream," he answered.

"But how did you – I don't understand?"

"We'll get around to that later...maybe. But for now, you have something that is very important to me. Something I lost last night."

"The coin! That was you last night at my window," Robbie said. "But how did you – and how did you know I had it?"

"You were rubbing it," answered Bonki. "That's what makes it work. That's why you had such a marvelous dream, and that's how I came to find it." He saw the puzzled look on Robbie's face. "More I can get around to explaining later...maybe. So can I have it? Please?"

"Sure," said Robbie, passing it through the window. Bonki accepted it into his teeny hand.

"It's a very pretty coin. What do the pictures and writing mean?" Robbie asked.

"Moon to stars, stars to moon. Rubbing the coin unites the two. Sometimes, and with a true heart, making the impossible - possible. If the big guy knew that I had been so careless with it, why I'm not sure what he'd do."

"The big guy?" asked Robbie

"Yeah, you know…Santa."

"Santa," Robbie repeated. "You mean he's real?"

"As real as I am. How real am I?" Bonki asked. With that, Robbie slowly reached through the window again to touch Bonki's nose.

 "Honk!" shouted Bonki. Robbie flinched.

"Quiet! – you'll wake my Mom and Dad," he snapped.

"Oh, they can't hear us," replied his new friend. "Something else I'll get around to – never mind. I probably won't get around to explaining that one. Anyway, I've been slipping with my responsibilities, and this is most likely my last year to be part of the Big Show.

"The Big Show?" asked Robbie.

"Christmas Eve." I've never lost my coin before, nor have I ever been seen by any boy or girl. Getting older, I guess."

"But you look so young," Robbie responded.

"Yeah, not bad for 274, I guess. But time to step aside, and make room for someone younger. The guy next in line for my position is barely 100. I just wanted to get one last year under my belt. And the big guy said it would be ok. But if he knew I lost my coin – "

"Oh, I would never tell, honest."

"You're a good boy, Robbie. And I know that you're having a rough time since the move. That's why I was here last night. Checking on you. He sends us out on special missions, now and then."
"But how did you - I know, you'll explain later."

"Probably not, but you're catching on," replied Bonki. "So what did you ask the big guy for, this Christmas?"

"I didn't," answered Robbie.

"Really? Why?" asked Bonki.

"Wasn't sure I believed in this anymore."

"Well, at least we put that doubt to rest…yes?"

"Duh!" answered Robbie.

"Ok, I'm the next best thing to Santa," boasted Bonki. "I'm sure you'll get plenty of nice gifts, but what is the one gift you want more than anything?"

"Not sure," answered Robbie. "I guess with everything going on, I never really thought about it."

"Well, I'll tell you what. Since you found my coin and saved my Christmas, I am going to do my best to save yours. There are only two days until Christmas Eve, but I want you to think real hard about what you truly want. And I give you my word as an Elf, that I will return tomorrow night for your answer." "So you really are an Elf," Robbie stated.

"Duh!" Bonki answered, with a smile. Just then, Robbie was alarmed by a noise from the hallway outside his door. And when he returned his attention to the window again, Bonki was gone. Robbie stepped to the edge of his bed and stuck his head through the window. He looked over the yard, and then confirmed quietly to himself – "Tomorrow night."

The next day, Robbie did nothing but think hard about what he wanted for Christmas. A part of him wanted so badly for night to come, and to see his new friend again. And the other part of him labored feverishly, trying to come up with the one gift that would mean more to him than anything else. He had been to several stores with his Mother, the day before. And even though he had seen at least a hundred new and exciting toys, nothing he saw would be special enough to him. And it was when he obeyed his Mother's wishes and continued going through the boxes in his room that Robbie came across a picture of him and his best buds, Todd and Mike. He sat on the floor, and his eyes started to water. Moments later, he stopped and pulled up his shirt to dry his eyes. Then, with the photo still in hand, he turned to the window and smiled.

That night, Robbie laid in bed patiently staring at his window. Praying that it hadn't all just been some beautiful, elaborate dream. His eyes moved to the red digital numbers of his clock on the dresser, and back to the window again, anticipating the visit that was promised to him. This went on for what seemed like forever when his 8-year-old body finally gave in, and Robbie fell asleep.

Tap tap tap!

Robbie opened his eyes to find Bonki smiling in his window. He then quickly looked at his clock and noticed it was 1:15 in the morning.

"I didn't think you were coming," said Robbie, while sliding his window open.

"I gave you an Elf's promise," answered Bonki. "Only I never said what time I'd be here. Very busy time for us, you know."

"I get it," said Robbie.

"Well? What did you come up with? Anything you want" stated Bonki. With that, Robbie held up a picture he had been holding on to all night. The very same picture he had found earlier that day. He stared at it for a brief moment and then presented it to Bonki.

"What is this?" Bonki asked.

"This is what I want. I want my best friends again. I want how it was before," Robbie replied, his eyes starting to tear up, once again.

"Oh, Robbie. I don't know," replied Bonki, losing his smile for the first time since they met.

"You said anything. You can do this…you're magic!" Robbie said when he started to cry. After that, Bonki crawled through the window and took a seat next to Robbie on the edge of his bed. He looked up into Robbie's eyes and placed a tiny hand on Robbie's arm.

"Robbie, I don't think you understand how difficult that would be. What you're asking for, why that's not a gift - that would be a miracle. Miracles do happen, but you need to understand something, Robbie. Sometimes in the midst of what would appear to be something terrible, can emerge something really great. A hidden miracle, if you will." He then paused for a moment. "I will give it my best."

"An elf's promise?" asked Robbie.

"An elf's promise," answered Bonki. That being said, Bonki leaped to his feet and moved to the window.

"Wait!" shouted Robbie. Bonki turned around. "There's something I've been wanting to ask."

"What is it?" asked Bonki.

"Do elves really have pointy ears?" Bonki smiled and lifted the left side of his hair, revealing a tiny, but normal ear.

"Who comes up with that stuff?" he said. They both laughed, and Bonki shoved one leg through the window. He looked to Robbie one last time, before committing to his exit.

"Remember what I told you," Bonki said.

"I will," replied Robbie.

"Oh, and Robbie…Merry Christmas."

"Same to you," said Robbie. Then, just as sudden as the mysterious new friend had entered Robbie's life, he was now gone. Robbie went to close his window and became mesmerized by the moon's brilliant glow. A single tear ran down his left cheek, and he knew he would most likely never see his new friend again. "Merry Christmas, Bonki," he whispered, just before sliding the window shut.

Another day came and went, and then it was Christmas Eve. Glorious Christmas Eve. His encounter with Bonki definitely made him more accepting of it all again. Whether it was the anticipation of his wish coming true, or finally giving in to the realization that this was indeed the Eve of the greatest day of a kid's year, Robbie was excited. How could he not be? Tomorrow was Christmas day! And with everything he now knew, it was magical once again. His family went through the day of festivities they were accustomed to doing, and it wasn't long before Robbie found himself sitting at the table, finishing his single glass of egg nog. This would be the very last thing he would do before climbing into bed and then trying his hardest to go to sleep.

And that is exactly what he did. He laid there, thinking of everything he had encountered the past few nights, and of his new mystical friend. He thought about everything they talked about, and especially the last thing Bonki said to him. What did it mean? He thought and thought until his brain finally could think no more. He yawned, turned to take one last look at his window, and did the unthinkable. On Christmas Eve…little Robbie Baron finally went to sleep.

"Robbie. Wake up, Robbie."

Robbie's eyes popped open, and he sat up to look at his window. Bonki wasn't there. No one was there. But there was something, and it was now calling for his attention. Robbie rubbed his eyes and moved to the window. There on the windowsill sat a small box wrapped in shiny red foil paper and tied with a white silk bow. It appeared to almost glow in the moonlight. He immediately knew it was for him, and he needed only one guess to know who it was from. Robbie's hands shook as he carefully unwrapped the box, and proceeded to open it. Inside the box, he found a small leather pouch and a note.

The note read: *Hello Robbie, I did my very best to honor your wish. But no matter the outcome, I wanted you to have my coin. I feel it is only right that you should have it, now that I no longer have a need for it. And who knows, there may still be a little magic left. You are a good boy, Robbie. And my wish to you is that you have a Christmas you will never forget. Merry Christmas! Your friend, Bonki*

Robbie's heart was beating faster as he un-cinched the pouch, letting the beautiful antique coin drop into his hand. He looked at his clock and saw that it was only a little past 2 am. As beautiful as the wrapped box was, he buried it deep into the trash. He then hid his note and crawled back into bed with his coin. He laid there rubbing the coin until he finally was able to fall back to sleep.

Christmas morning had come, and Bonki was right. Robbie opened several very nice gifts. He even got a brand new sled. But nothing that even came close to giving any indication that his wish would come true.

"I don't know what I was expecting?" he quietly mumbled.

"What honey?" his Mom asked.

"Nothing."

"Hey, I was talking to our new neighbors, and they said there's a big hill that all the kids sled down…just a few yards over. After breakfast, why don't you take your new sled and check it out?" his Dad announced.

The walk only took 10 minutes, and Robbie found himself standing at the top of the hill. There was a fresh dusting of snow and not another soul around. He smiled and jetted down for his first run. By the time he made his way back to the top again, he was met by two other kids.

"Hi I'm Jason, and this is my sister, Alley."

"I'm Robbie. We just moved here."

"That's cool!" Jason replied.

"Cool sled," said Alley.

"Ok, we'll stand on our sleds and see who makes it the furthest, before losing our balance and falling off," announced Jason.

"Cool!" said Robbie. They spent the next couple of hours laughing and playing, and really getting to know each other. And as he watched his new friends race down the hill, he all at once understood what Bonki meant by 'a hidden miracle'. His lesson was all too clear to Robbie now, and he knew he had gotten the best gift of all. But he also knew he could never try to tell anyone about his experience, and of his new mystical friend who had come to him in the night. No one would ever begin to understand. Heck, so much of it he still didn't understand. Especially since there were so many unanswered questions. But then a feeling came to him that maybe would explain everything. Maybe, just maybe, those questions are better left unanswered. Maybe that's the magic that makes Christmas so great. He saw Jason running towards him.

"Hey, do you think you can meet us back here tomorrow too? My cousin Todd, and his buddy Mike are supposed to come over."

"You're kidding," Robbie blurted out.

"What?"

"Nothing. Yeah...yeah, I'll be here," he quickly answered.

"Cool! They're bringing their sleds, and we'll probably build a snow fort or something."

"That sounds great!" Robbie said as an anxious chill rushed through him.

"Cool! Well, we gotta head back home now...being Christmas and all. See you later."

"See ya!" Robbie shouted as he watched Jason and Alley run for home, pulling their sleds close behind. Robbie pulled off his glove, dug his hand deep into his right front pocket, and returned it with the coin. He began to rub it, all the while smiling, when he then said out loud – "Now you're just showing off!" And as Robbie too headed home, it would seem that Bonki's wish had also come true. For this would, without a doubt, be the Christmas Robbie would never forget.

"Nothing's as mean as giving a little child something useful for Christmas."

–Kin Hubbard

"I haven't taken my Christmas lights down. They look so nice on the pumpkin."

– Winston Spear

"Most of the soap operas always use the Christmas special to kill huge quantities of their characters. So they have trams coming off their rails, or cars slamming into each other or burning buildings. It's a general clean-out."

Brooke Stang

Brooke Stang lives with her two daughters and husband in the Midwest. She loves going on adventures with her young family. She adopted a black and white cat, Sergeant Peppermint after her daughter fell in love with him at the shelter.

She has written seven books to date; one was hastily published on Amazon under Adalynn Rafe. She graduated with an Associates of Science and studied Biotechnology. Writing and science will always be her lifelong passions.

Granite Giants

A short story by Brooke Stang

Based on true events

Everyone aspires to be somebody, to do something, to be better than the generation before them. It could be in terms of making a career, being a better parent, leaving an area, and starting new somewhere else. Whatever that aspiration is, it's there. Deep down inside the human soul, we all aspire to be something more.

What happens when new aspirations collide with old aspirations. Can we be the kids with big dreams, staring at the stars, wishing to land on Mars and be our adult selves stuck in reality?

To me, I left that kid at home when I grew up. I moved away. I left familiarity in search of something more. When I left, I closed a chapter to open a new one, but I never finished the previous chapter.

Now, while hiking where I once traveled so many times before, it felt alien. Foreign. I had hiked here, snowshoed here, snowboarded, and climbed giant boulders made of granite. This was my backyard, the place I escaped to dream big dreams.

Now…now I was a foreigner.

The new me walked parallel to an old me this Christmas season. That laughing girl trudging through mud didn't have the same spirit as the woman I was now, hiking through snow and ice. I barely recognized that girl anymore, even as I stared directly at her—her hair a wild orange mane poking out of her hood, a freckled face, and chapped lips. How she lived for adventure! She was me once upon a time, but that girl was just a memory.

Christmas of late brought out anxiety and depression. It wasn't a matter of returning to my childhood home, seeing extended family, or catching up with friends. Usually, that restored some sort of holiday cheer. My inner *bah-humbug* was different. It was a pain in my chest when I looked at the woman in the mirror.

In my reflection, I saw a weathered woman, beaten down by life, barely scraping by day to day. I saw a mother who loved her children, a wife that loved her husband, but I didn't see the hope or excitement that once occupied her eyes.

A cold breeze brought me back to the present, back to the forest. Everything was still and quiet, besides the occasional vehicle driving through the canyon. I breathed in deeply, exhaling a cloud of vapor. The air tasted different here—polluted, almost. It was a testament that the city below had grown past its limits. Everything everywhere changed eventually.

This old canyon was different in the winter. There was no foliage separating the path from the sky above. During the day the sun would beat down and reflect off the snow, blinding anyone trying to hike. At sunset, the sunlight sparkled pink and orange across the ice crystals, absorbing the gorgeous colors casted by the smoggy air of the Great Smokey Valley

Knotted limbs of old oak trees mixed with white trunks of aspens. Granite giants slept, curled up as boulders the size of houses. Pine trees housed critters and sheltered the trail from the bitterly cold elements. The main trail followed the river. In some areas the land sloped straight down, exposing giant tree roots and protruding rocks topped with crystal clear ice.

The main path was compacted and icy from use. It was unlike the clean, crisp snow I had forged my way through in the forest. It was slippery and unstable; I regretted not bringing crampons or trekking poles.

I hiked uphill, past a small waterfall that poured through a hole in the ice. When the spring runoff happened, this entire trail would flood. The river would have enough force to move two-ton boulders miles down the river bank. In the winter it was merely a creek dancing through a bed of icy blue granite and iron-ringed sandstone.

It was analogous to human life. Once upon a time, I had so many opportunities drowning me. Now, life was a steady trickle of water. The seasons of my aspirations had changed.

It reminded me of the one Christmas that changed my life:

Mom brought home a hitchhiker. With her sister, she had traveled to attend the funeral of one of their half-sisters on their father's side. On the way home, they picked up a man that was walking in a blizzard. He was cold and hungry. I was young, only a child of maybe seven or eight.

I remember my mom feeding this stranger a warm meal, offering a hot bath, and allowing him to sort through my dad's old clothes. After that, I accompanied my parents to the homeless shelter downtown, about a thirty-minute drive from our cozy suburb life.

I was at a stage in my life where I was very angry. Being the middle of five children, my mom recently being ill with a debilitating head injury, going through my own personal trauma (that would be locked away and kept secret for another twenty years)—I had a "why me" mentality. I didn't care about the needs or wants of anyone else, especially not my siblings. There was just so much anger surrounding everything I did.

We dropped this man at the homeless shelter. It was just me and my beloved parents. They drove an old Ford Windstar—champagne-colored, not brown. Instead of going right back to the freeway, my parents drove through the darkest parts of town... the parts of town that no one wanted to acknowledge or fix. They were the parts of town that housed hundreds if not thousands of souls that had lost their way in life.

These people lived under overpasses, surviving on liquor and tire fires. Bodies lie motionless on the sides of the roads. Feet poked out of the ends of large boxes. How many of those bodies were lifeless and dead and how many struggled to survive?

My little heart shattered into a million pieces when I saw this.

I remember bawling. I remember telling my parents to take Christmas back and give it to these people that had no home, no warmth, and no suburban cushy life.

My feet scraped along the icy trail. My lips pursed and I gulped back a wad of emotion. My ankles felt tired and sore from hiking on uneven ice and snow. In my head I pictured a child crying, wishing, praying for strangers she'd never met. I could still see the headlights of cars passing by, the droplets of water on the windshield, snow melted by the heater that blew against the glass. I could hear the whoosh of tires through slushy streets.

With a sniffle, I continued up the uneven trail. My nose and cheeks stung from the cold, my eyes watered from the chilly breeze. My thumb pressed against my fingers, now balled into a fist to keep warm in my sleeve. I hadn't even brought gloves. It would be dark in less than a half-hour, but I kept going.

Impulsivity would eventually be my downfall.

On this path, I was merging my two selves. The girl that had a million dreams and the woman who barely made it day by day were meeting each other, realizing that they were one.

I passed more sleeping giants curled up as boulders made of granite. We used to try to climb them using the lanky oak trees that surrounded them. I was never good at rock climbing. My strength was in my legs and hips, not my arms or back. I was also the cautious child—always watching and constantly observing. Over the years I had found great pride in my ability to merely watch a situation without getting caught up in it.

Finally, I reached my destination. It was an old pavilion set up in the early twentieth century. The quarry workers used it as a rest station when mining the granite from this canyon to build the city below. Somehow, they'd drill hundreds of holes into the rock, fill the holes with water, and allow it to freeze. The expansion of the ice was enough to break the rock from the canyon walls. It was a tactic that relied on the power of numbers.

In it's prime, this pavilion was a godsend to exhausted miners. It's where they'd refuel and reset before returning to work climbing boulders the size of small homes and cliff faces that offered certain death in the event of uneven footing.

Once the mining was completed, the pavilion was abandoned. My grandmother remembered having dances in the canyon when she was a teenager. Now it was forgotten. Graffitied. Crumbling away.

In one corner was a fireplace, not that it was used as such anymore. I knew they'd done renovations at some point, judging by the stark contrast in materials. An old foundation of stone and mortar had been laid over with concrete. Solid steel beams kept the roof up, which was now made of hammered metal. It was the size of a modest living room, but nothing fancy. It was just an old abandoned shelter.

I used to think that graffiti was so ugly and desecrating. It wasn't until I was in my mid-twenties that I realized that graffiti told a story. I started looking at graffiti on train cars, abandoned buildings, even canyon walls as story pieces—visualizations with little explanation.

There was once a graffitied rock in a nature reserve that was built right where the highway split apart. It became a landmark to the area. When the nature reserve was cleaned up and a new bridge over the freeway was made, the rock was gone. Decades of stories through vandalism had been taken away overnight.

It was a reminder that nothing lasted forever.

The air got colder as the sun set further toward the western mountain range. In the middle of the concrete floor were burnt logs and ash—evidence of many fires that kept people warm on their mountain journey.

I decided it was time to head back. My toes were cold, and lips chapped. I had left my cellphone in my car so that I could think without distraction. On my hike way up, I slipped plenty of times; I knew I'd slip twice that going down, especially as it got darker.

As I hiked, I remembered a more recent Christmas.

My oldest was two. My husband was unemployed. We lived off my retail wage of twelve dollars an hour and occasional handouts from our parents. Each time I called Mom and Dad for help a part of my independence died. I hated having to ask my parents for grocery money or help with rent. My parents were always eager and happy to help me. They were in a place financially that they could help. Yet, it still battered my ego and destroyed my pride.

One day I broke down. I posted on social media that I was too poor to keep the pots and pans I had bought myself for Christmas that year. Even after working nonstop and rarely getting to see my daughter, I still couldn't afford the much-needed pots and pans. I didn't dare ask my parents for more; they'd given us so much.

At that point in our marriage, I was about to break. I had always been good at running away when things got too hard. It was a coping tactic I learned growing up. One snap and I'd retreat into the far reaches of my psyche and hide. What would emerge was a mean and awful girl in survival mode. I was like a cat with claws that had been tortured—hissing, scratching, and fighting until the environment was safe again. It took many years of therapy to fix this little hissing cat-child and begin a healing relationship with myself.

I held on through that storm because I knew that storms do not last. My husband had a rough time finding employment and I just had to have faith that things would work out. Eventually, he found a job, and we got back up on our feet. It was a very rough patch but looking back, I was glad I didn't give up on us.

It was during that chaotic Christmas that we heard a knock on our door. On the doorstep was Santa's bag filled with breads, meats, and various treats. A box sat beside it. Inside was goodies for our daughter—a coloring book, hat and gloves, and a few small toys. It was from a group of strangers.

 I later found it came from some of our church members. It wasn't a large flashy expensive gift, and that's why it meant so much. After working retail, I had seen how superficial the holidays had become. It felt like we lived in a culture that treasured possessions over people sometimes.

This little bit of Christmas giving really brought some much-needed love and light to a very dark year. I'd never forgotten that snowy, blessed day.

Off the beaten path I found my footprints, the only set in the forest snow. It was almost like they were waiting for my return. How many times had I hiked this path, taken this unmarked trail, but never left any mark behind? Before me was a reminder of who I'd been years ago and who I was today.

I stepped into the footprint, my feet facing forward in a now backward print.

This is who I am.

Trudging through the snow and back through the quiet forest, I made it to my car and back down the canyon.

I reflected on a woman that acknowledged her youthful dreams while living in the present. Once I dreamed about setting foot on Mars, of becoming a great scientist and curing rare diseases, and making my name as an author.

I knew what my real dreams were. They greeted me at the door and called me mom. They were in the tender kiss from my dear husband.

My old dreams and aspirations would make me a better woman. I'd know what to say when my own girls came to me, telling me they wanted to visit a far-off planet or become a fashion designer. I would know what to say because I was once that girl.

I realized that the places I had been, the events that had unfolded around me, and the lives that not only I impacted but had also impacted me made me who I was today. The twenty-year-old me had no clue what was actually in store for her.

This Christmas I didn't ask for anything, yet I found everything.

It was right before me all along.

"What I like about Christmas is that you can make people forget the past with the present."

— Don Marquis

"If you can't wrap Christmas presents well, at least make it look like they put up a good fight."

— Author Unknown

Some Christmas tree ornaments do more than glitter and glow, they represent a gift of love given a long time ago."

--Tom Baker

Anne Petrous

Anne Petrous is an amateur author who writes for fun when she has time. Publications include community cookbooks, Reunions Magazine, The Beacon NewsMagazine and ((Ring Ring)) Hello? Grandma's House, Big Bad Wolf Speaking – A Christmas Anthology Part One. She is also a former co-host of That Damn Radio Show.

Currently, she is an Assistant Harbor Master at a local marina; she enjoys spending time with her family – especially her grandchildren and her two dogs.

Charlotte's Magical Adventure

By Anne Petrous

Summer was over and fall has arrived. This was Charlotte's favorite time of year; not because school has started and she missed her friends over the summer, but because the weather was beginning to change. The leaves began to change color as they floated gently to the ground in the crisp, cool breeze.

Halloween was just around the corner; while the excitement of dressing up as a pirate or a princess and trick or treating around the neighborhood would be fun, it was the next holiday that Charlotte loved most. For she knew, just a few short weeks after Thanksgiving would be Christmas!

Charlotte knew her Christmas friend, Snickerdoodle (Snicker for short), would arrive on Thanksgiving. "I wonder how Snicker will arrive this year?" she thought. Last year, Snicker arrived by hot air balloon; the year before, she flew in on a reindeer.

As Charlotte was watching the parade, the smell of roasted turkey filled the air. Suddenly, an arrow zoomed past Charlotte, followed by a glittery thin rope. Snicker soon followed sliding down the rope and let go, just above Charlotte, and landed in her lap.

Snicker asked Charlotte if she had been good all year, she replied "Oh yes, I've been very good! I helped around the house and I also helped with my baby brother." Charlotte knew that if she had been good all year and helped out around the house, Snicker would have a very special surprise for her this year.

Charlotte was curious all year, often wondering what the surprise would be….maybe a new baby doll – one that can open and close its eyes. She received a toy kitchen for her birthday, maybe it would be accessories for it or a chef hat with an apron with her name embroidered on it. Charlotte wanted to ask but knew she had to wait. Snicker wanted to make a game of it and leave a couple of clues to see if Charlotte would be able to figure it out.

When she awoke the next morning, she looked out her bedroom window and saw sparkly snow and snowmen – that waved to her! She thought that was a neat surprise, but little did she know, that was not the surprise. Later that evening, she spotted a reindeer in her backyard. Now she was really curious. When she awoke the next morning, her room looked different, and she began to tell Snicker about the crazy dream she had about riding on a reindeer through the starry night as sparkling snow fell from the sky - then she realized she was not at home! It wasn't a dream, she really rode on a reindeer, but where was she?

"Come on, follow me!" Snicker exclaimed excitedly. As they walked down the hallway, Charlotte couldn't help but notice all the portraits of Santa Claus, Mrs. Claus, reindeers, and elves. Snicker giggled and told her to hurry up; they don't want to be late. They were going to meet someone very special.

At the end of the hall was a large arched shaped wood door that had beautiful carved winter scenes. Charlotte slowly opened the door and gasped as she saw elves hurrying around in what seemed to be a small village. She saw a bakery and soon smelled the delicious aroma of the cookies and cakes. They stopped for a cup of hot cocoa complete with snowflake-shaped marshmallows. They passed by a chocolate store, a candy store, a music store that only played Christmas music, and several other boutiques that she planned on checking out before she went home. As they continued down the street, she saw a large building that looked like a giant toy box. "Is that…no, it can't be….is that Santa's workshop?" she asked Snicker. Snicker giggled and winked her eye. As they climbed the steps, Santa opened the door and he stepped outside. "HO HO HO, it is so very nice to meet you Charlotte, Snicker has told me what a good little girl you have been, I just had to meet you in person," he said. Charlotte still couldn't believe where she was or who she was with. "Is this real? Or am I dreaming" she asked? Just then, an elf snuck up behind her, giggled, and pinched her, "OUCH! I really am awake!" Charlotte giggled.

As they walked around the workshop, Santa explained what the elves where doing; some were making toys, some were designing toys, there were a few writing new stories, designing new puzzles, creating new games and one of Snickers' friends was drawing pictures for a special coloring book. As the elves were busy making toys, one began to sing *"Tap, tap, tap, goes my little hammer, Ring, ring, goes my little bell, we are Santa's helpers, making Christmas toys."* Soon everyone joined in.

The next stop was the reindeer barn, they were practicing takeoffs and landings. There were a couple of elves in the meadow throwing snowballs at each other while some polar bears decorated the evergreen trees.

Charlotte was getting hungry and as they began to walk to Santa's chalet, she noticed the aroma of gingerbread….she could almost taste it. Mrs. Clause had a fire in the fireplace and a small table set up with fresh-baked gingerbread cookies and hot cocoa with whipped cream and crushed peppermints on top. As they began some small talk, they strung up some popcorn and cranberries and wrapped them around a tree.

It began to snow (again – that happens a lot at the North Pole)…the most sparkly snow you ever saw…so magical, it really was because it only landed on the rooftops, trees and grass! The walkways stayed clear! Charlotte knew she would have to go home soon, but she wanted to see as much as she could. She heard some laughter in the distance and began to run towards it. She saw the most amazing skating rink; she had never seen an outdoor rink before. The ice was so smooth and shiny, almost mirror-like. One of the elves handed her a pair of skates and she began skating around the rink with all the elves, "this is so much fun," she thought.

 It was beginning to get late, and even though Charlotte was having a good time and making many new friends, she started to miss her baby brother and the rest of her family. Charlotte and Snicker climbed aboard Santa's mini sleigh (he used this sleigh for short trips), hooked up 4 reindeer, and off they went. The moon was full, almost a silvery color, in the dark blue sky. Charlotte opened up the picnic basket Chef Elf packed for the trip…hot cocoa and cookies, both still warm and freshly made. Through the night time sky, they flew, in and out of clouds, the bright stars guiding them all the way.

Christmas soon arrived and there was a very special gift for Charlotte and her baby brother… hand-sewn stockings with their names embroidered on them, made by Mrs. Claus! Each one was decorated differently and filled with small toys, candies, cookies, storybooks, coloring books, and crayons. The storybooks told about Charlotte's adventure and the coloring books were drawings of her adventure so she could color and relive her adventures over and over. She often told her baby brother about her adventure and told him, if he was good like her and helped around the house, maybe, just maybe, Snicker would tell Santa and he would be able to take a magical trip to the North Pole too! Baby Andy smiled and laughed with a twinkle in his eye.

"Oh look, yet another Christmas TV special! How touching to have the meaning of Christmas brought to us by cola, fast food, and beer... Who'd have ever guessed that product consumption, popular entertainment, and spirituality would mix so harmoniously?"

– Bill Watterson, Calvin & Hobbes

"I hate Christmas. The mall is full of nothing but women and children. All you hear is, 'I want this,' 'Get me this,' 'I have to have this'... and then there's the children. And they're all by my store 'cause they stuck the mall Santa right outside ringing his stupid bell. As if you need a bell to notice a 300-pound alcoholic in a red suit. 'Ho, ho, ho,' all day long. So, nice as can be, I go outside, ask him to shut the hell up. He takes a swing at me. So I lay a hook into his fat belly and he goes down. Beard comes off, all the kids start crying and I'm the bad guy."

– Al Bundy in *Married With Children*

Alex Costea

I am Alex Costea, husband of Mary and father of Alex IV and Benjamin

I am an ordained UMC pastor, serving a 2-point charge in Western Oklahoma, having served in the pulpit since 1993. I have served 7 charges in OKLA (churches) since my first appointment.

I have an AAS in Biology from Eastern State College (Wilburton, OK) - my BS is from Southeastern Okla State Univ. (Durant, OK) in Biology, Chemistry, English, and Sociology. I also studied Education at OK Panhandle State Univ (Goodwell, OK)

I have an M.Div from Phillips Theological Seminary (Tulsa, OK) with specializations in Church History and general Theology

I grew up in the Washington DC area (Fairfax VA) and graduated from JEB Stuart HS in 1972.

I am a USAF veteran (1972 - 82) and was in Telecommunications Operations and was a Military Training Instructor (MTI).

THE CARD

By Alex Costea

Suffice it to say, that up until 1984, I had been on a course of self-destruction that came into full bloom.

By the time I left high school in 1972, I was a full-blown alcoholic but managed to hide it pretty well when I joined the Air Force in June of that year. After a very interesting, but undistinguished – if shortened – career, I was given my walking papers in 1982. In fact, the only honorable thing I really did was accept that discharge.

Not long after that, my wife decided that she had put up with enough of me, and gave me a dishonorable discharge in 1984. She moved out, with our then 5-year-old son – and truthfully, I don't remember a thing about that. I had become a desperate, sick, and broken-down drunk, and she was right to dump me.

Somehow I managed to make it – with all my belongings stuffed into a VW "bug" from San Antonio, Texas to Ponca City, Oklahoma – to the apartment of a friend from my USAF days who was working there. For the roughly 2-weeks I was there with him, he later told me that I was the terror of the apartment building, and all I did was drink. I am not sure what else I may have done during that time, because it is all still a blackout blur.

Needless to say, my stay in Oklahoma was not pleasant, because one day in September 1984 I "woke up" in the Kay County jail with no idea how I got there, or what I was in that cell for. It wasn't long before a jailer came to my cell to check on me – that whole story is for another page – and I had the opportunity to ask "how long they keep someone in the drunk tank?" I was under no illusion about my life as a drunk and assumed that was the reason for my presence there.

He replied that the "drunk tank" was on the other side of the jail area, and they only put folk with a felony charge or major misdemeanor charge in the area where I found myself. He said that I would be seeing my attorney that afternoon, and I could get the details from him.

Not long after lunch, I met my lawyer, and he told me that I was looking at a 5-years-to-life charge – and I was stunned. He then told me that I had committed a major 1st-degree felony and that I'd be seeing the judge for arraignment the next day.

Life became a blur of endless days, and in November of 1984, I stood in front of Judge Page and entered a "No Contest" plea. I was sentenced to 10 years, with a combination of prison time and probation. On 7 December 1984, I became inmate 142284 in the Oklahoma Department of Corrections, where I would be for the next 3 years.

Over those years, I managed to survive a few death threats and fights – common on the yard – and made it to house arrest (something they told me I'd never do). I was able to go to work and then to VoTech, which led to a small college scholarship. For the next few years, my life revolved around AA meetings, a few friends and books, while I worked thru to a Bachelor's Degree in Biology.

During that time, I had met and married a great Okie gal, and our lives soon took on a new dimension as I began work as a lay United Methodist Campus Minister. I was still taking Education classes, in the hopes of building up my academic record to where I could realistically apply for Graduate school, or go into teaching, but I guess that God had other ideas.

Soon, I ended up at a real church as a Pastor, and in Seminary, heading toward Ordination in the United Methodist Church. We had a son – Benjamin – during that time, and between school, church, and a new family, it was a struggle. But we managed to make things work, and family life was really pretty good.

Christmas of 1997, we had gone to her parent's house in Oklahoma City, and when we got back to Tulsa, where I was serving as a Student Pastor, I realized that I had forgotten to stop the mail.

The box was crammed with envelopes, so after I got my wife and son into the house, and he was busy with his new toys, I started to get things out of the car. There was one card with a San Antonio return address, and I knew that it could not be from my ex.

"Open the cards," I said to her as I went to collect another load. When I came back in, she was sitting on the kitchen floor, sobbing with a sort-of smile on her face. I asked what was wrong, and she tearily handed me the card. I looked at the note inside, and my tired heart soared!

It was from the son I last saw when he was aged 5, as he was leaving my life – I thought forever. He told me in that note that when he graduated from High School that May, he wanted to come visit me! What a Christmas present!

Fast forward a few days, after I had written him a letter in return, I got a call from him late one night, and I "met" my oldest son – again.

When he came to visit, we passed each other in the Tulsa airport, but soon were drawn to each other in a hug which only God could have arranged. From that time, through his graduation from 'boot camp" at Ft. Sill in Lawton, OK, through his time in the Army Guard and some deployments to the "big sandbox" of Iraq, we have grown closer as father and son.

I have his card framed on my office wall, and when I feel the need for a touch of God, all I have to do is look at it, and I am refreshed just like on that cold December night when I held it the first time.

Only God could have brought him and me thru this mess of my creation. But He knew that we would need each other, and saw to it that this prodigal father got a second chance to be the dad he always wanted to be. Both of my sons are friends now and share common interests in video gaming and weird movies.

And I am truly blessed – thanks to an unexpected, but very welcome Christmas card.

Miriam van der Duyn-Verijzer

My name is Miriam van der Duyn-Verijzer. I am 57 years of age and, married to Willem, mother of 3 wonderful children: Emmeke (33), Rob, (31), and Jasper (27), grandmother of a beautiful little girl Eydis (3). I'm so proud of them all!

I'm a teacher, started in 1985 as a kindergarten teacher. Later I taught also older groups. I worked as an art- and culture coordinator, I ensured that the art- and culture lessons were brought into the schools. I also worked in the library for the schools.

Nowadays I work as a teacher in secondary education. I teach students who have to learn Dutch. They come from different countries, such as Syria, Afghanistan, Eritrea, where there are war and hunger. But also to ex-pats from countries in Europe.
After this school, they can move on to regular education, so they must be able to speak and write Dutch well after 2 years.

This is a challenging job and I love it!

This is my story about my family, my memories, and a family bond that will never be broken.

But first I have to tell you more about my background and the reason why I want to write this. My parents passed away 4 years ago-only 23 days apart, and even now, I have still questions I wish I could ask them. So, this little story is for my children and grandchildren to understand why we celebrate Christmas as we do as a Verijzer-de Haas.

Born in 1963, the world was smaller than all our young ones can imagine. Communication went by writing a letter to family abroad, the telephone was seldom used, only in desperate times.
And when you wanted to visit people, you were lucky when you owned a car. My family comes from Vlissingen, a province in Zeeland, the Netherlands.

The year 1963 was a year full of sorrow and grief because my grandmother became very ill. Taking care of and looking after her own mother (my great grandmother) who died a couple of months before my birth, took its toll and she died only a couple of months after my birth. My mother never spoke about these difficult times she surely must have gone through. Missing your mother at such a young age she was only 30, being a young mom.

Who do you turn to with your questions? Before my birth, my mom was a teacher, just like my granddad and my great aunt. My father was a marine engineer. His employer promised him to be able to be with my mom during the weeks before and after my birth. Unfortunately, the employer didn't keep his promise and my father decided to end his job right then. What a brave and loving decision! In that year my father went to Nijmegen, 200 km from Vlissingen. Because my mom and I still lived in

Vlissingen, my birth town, they decided to move to Nijmegen in 1965 where my younger-little brother (born in 1966) and I grew up.

My earliest memories start in Nijmegen. My parents, torn away from their beloved family, friends, and birth town, started a new life in a very new part of the city. Lots of young families and young children to play with. I was happy, had a very happy childhood but I bet my mom and dad were lonely some of the time.

My father had his job, he worked in shifts at the powerplant PGEM, but my mom (as it was normal at that time) was a stay-at-home-mom. Her days must have been empty because when she was pregnant with me, she had to quit her job as a teacher (also very common these days). I was one and a half years of age when we moved to Nijmegen, so I have no real recollection of Vlissingen and the family my parents surely missed.

My grandfather and my great-aunt came over as often as they could. My grandfather was very proud of me, he took me into nature all

the time and taught me the names of birds, plants, and trees. The photo I inserted is one of my most favorite memories with him. Walking in the 'Hatertse Vennen', he showed and taught me so many things! It's still vivid in my memory. One time we saw a woodpecker stuck in a tree. And another time we caught a firefly. After examining the little animal he put it in a matchbox for me. When I wanted to look at it the next day, he told me that it probably crawled out. Now I know he

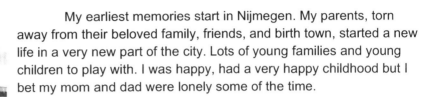

set it free at the moment I wasn't looking. He was the greatest animal lover in the world!

Also on holidays and of course at Christmastime my grandfather and my great aunt visited us. They stayed for a couple of weeks and went back home, or went to my mother's sister who lived with her family in Gravenhage to stay there for a couple of weeks. They never stayed at their own home for long.

My grandfather's family name is 'de Haas'. Translated: 'The Hare'. He always joked that he was royalty: 'Van Konijnenburcht tot Hazenstein'.

Translated it will be something like: 'From Rabbitscastle till Haretown'. That's one of the reasons why we eat rabbit for as long as I can remember on the first day of Christmas.

At the age of 4, I remember standing at the kitchen counter with my grandfather. On the shelf, there was a rabbit. My grandfather was cleaning the animal. Because I was curious, he showed me all the parts of the animal. In those days, rabbits weren't bred but shot in the fields. So after he stripped off his skin the first thing he explained was that we had to look for holes in the skin. I still remember that sound of skinning the rabbit! Then we examined the animal for hail shot. Then the belly from the skinny animal was sliced. All intestines came out. In the intestines, there were still droppings. It was really funny to see them pushed out. Heart, liver, kidneys, lungs, and even the brains were kept because they also were a part of dinner. The whole animal was used for the feast. Nowadays children don't know what it's like, preparing food like this.

My grandfather died when I was 7 years of age. Even though he isn't around me for a long time anymore, there are many occasions that I have to think of him. Or think I hear him, telling me what beautiful flower or bird that is. And in his legacy, our family's tradition is to gather at Christmas and eat rabbit.

In the passing years, more and more side dishes were added to the dinner. So, this isn't just a Christmas story, but also our recipe for a wonderful meal together with not only family but also with friends. Because friends are the family closer to our hearts than some of our near family members. Since my mom passed away, I took over the tradition and prepared this dish already 4 times. And I will keep up doing this, till my days are over and my children will take over from me (I hope).

Preparation of the rabbit:

Start preparing the rabbit at least 2 days in advance. Take as many rabbit legs you need: 1 per person is the least. Use butter as well as oil (but not too much, watch out for fat splashes!) For seasoning, you only need salt and pepper.

Sear them in a large pan until the skin is crispy brown. Then add water, the legs must be submerged. Also, add some bay leaf and whole peppercorns. Let this simmer on the stove for at least a couple of hours. Make sure that the water does not boil down too much to prevent burning. Every time you check the rabbit, cover the rabbit with the gravy to keep it juicy. Repeat a couple of times a day

Start the next morning again and do the same, until the meat becomes falling off the bone. Then put the dish in the oven at a lower temperature to get it fully cooked. The rabbit is done when the meat comes off the bone without effort.

Side-dishes:

Potato croquettes from the oven, cranberry sauce, Brussels sprouts (stir-fry), homemade apple sauce from apples from our own garden, green beans, and delicious red wine to finish it off.

I hope you enjoyed my memories and the recipe of our family tradition!

Big hugs from the Netherlands and have a wonderful Christmas together.

Miriam van der Duyn-Verijzer -- October 2020

"I've learned that you can tell a lot about a person by the way he handles these three things: a rainy day, lost luggage, and tangled Christmas tree lights."

— Maya Angelou

"The worst gift is a fruitcake. There is only one fruitcake in the entire world, and people keep sending it to each other."

— Johnny Carson

6. "It's always consoling to know that today's Christmas gift are tomorrow's garage sales."

— Milton Berle

"We celebrate the birth of one who told us to give everything to the poor by giving each other motorized tie racks."

— Bill McKibben

Sue Veryser-Duncan

Sue Veryser was born and raised in Chesterfield Township, Michigan She has two brothers and two sisters, but lost her older brother in 2009 to a heart attack

Sue has been writing since she was nine, with her grandmother as her muse. Her grandmother would cut pictures out of gossip rags, tape them inside an old wallpaper book, then tape a piece of lined paper on the opposite side and say, "Look at the picture, now write me a story.

She has owned various newspapers and magazines since 1991. Her dream has always been writing books and owning her own book publishing company.

She says, "Everyone has a story to tell, and everyone's story needs and deserves to be told, and that is exactly what I am doing.

One Christmas Wish

By Sue Veryser-Duncan

It shows up out of nowhere — the burning tears, the empty feeling in the pit of my stomach — the reasserting of the knowledge that one of us will be missing this year, at Christmas.

For the part of the family that was at my parent's house for Thanksgiving, we've already experienced one holiday without him, but that doesn't mean that this Christmas will be any less sorrowful.

I had a dream, the other night, about him. He was laughing and telling stories, and I ran into his arms and said, "Oh Jerry! Thank God, it was only a bad dream." He gave me a huge hug, a big kiss, told me he loved me, and with his arm still slung over my shoulder, continued on with his amusing tales. It was so real. I could feel him, smell him.

I woke suddenly, to the sound of my dog barking to go outside. In that veil between dreams and awake, I was so happy to know that Jerry's death was just a bad dream. It never really happened, I told myself. I made a mental note to call him that day, to tell him of my silly dream.

I swung my feet over the side of the bed and as they touched the cold wood floor, reality swooped in, and sorrow quickly followed.

And every time I have that kind of dream, and every time I have to remember that he's gone, a piece of me dies with the dream. I wonder if there will ever be enough time to heal the wounds that his passing left behind — not mine in particular — but those of all whose lives he touched. I think it's probably this way for anyone who has ever lost someone close to them. I know I am not alone… still….

Christmas is here. I remember as kids, Mom and Dad always made me buy my brother's socks, for Christmas. I also remember how little enthusiasm was present in their actions as they were opened their present from me. As we grew older and started drawing names, it seemed I drew Jerry's name more often than not, and when I did I always bought him a pack of "Over the calf sweat socks" to go along with whatever it was he "really" wanted for Christmas.

I was shopping at Meijers, just yesterday, and without thinking, I steered my cart to the sock department, grabbed a pack of "over the calf sweat socks" and tossed them in the cart. It wasn't until I got to the self-checkout that I realized what I had done. I scanned all of my items while swiping at the unwanted tears that ran in steady streams, clouding my vision and doing a real number on my mascara.

As the emptiness of sorrow came in waves, I reached for the last item in the cart — the package of socks — and I hugged them to my chest. I am pretty sure no one saw me do this, but at that moment, I really didn't care.

I bought them. Not because I needed them, or wanted them, but because it made me feel better — made me feel like maybe someday, we will get to see him again. God, I hope we do. It's hard enough to know that we have to go the rest of our lives without that laugh and smile and LOVE — an eternity without that would be hell

So, although I hate those dreams — hate that moment when I have to face that fact that Jerry is gone, I don't want to stop having them, either — because while they are in progress, life is back to normal. The family is whole again. My parents are whole again. It's a precious moment, fragile and priceless — it has the magical properties where in one instant a wish has the possibility of coming true.

Mom said she has only one Christmas wish… "I want my kid back". I watched sadness wash over her, and the tears spring up and out as she made her announcement. And I held her and wept with her and dad. It is so hard to watch parents hurt and not be able to do anything to take the pain away. I suppose if you asked anyone in the family, what their one Christmas wish would be, it would be to have Jerry back, healthy, happy, and whole.

This year, I will still wish on the Christmas Star, and I will wish for just that one thing. For a brief moment, my inner child will believe that it is possible. And that is the one moment I hope to carry with me for the rest of my life.

Christmas is going to be rough, this year — one of us is missing — but if we're lucky enough, he'll show up in our dreams, and we can hug him, tell him that we love him, and carry him with us for the rest of our lives.

God Bless and may your Christmas Wish come true.

There is no such thing as the perfect Christmas Tree

By Sue Veryser-Duncan

Every year I set out to find it, and every year I end up with something that leans more towards Charlie Brown's stick with a bulb on it, rather than the grand Time Square image. And do not think that I use the word "lean" lightly, because last year -- well, let me start from the beginning.

Last year, Brian and I decided that we should have a real tree. It was our first Christmas together and we wanted it to be memorable. What's more memorable than going out to shop for a real tree? But, do we drive out to a tree farm and cut one down, or do we just go buy one that is already vivisected from its roots and looking for a home? That was the first question that we pondered, and it was immediately answered by my inner Tree Hugger, which pointed out that there was no sense in killing another tree when there were already so many dead ones standing, and laying around, in tree lots all over the city.

So off we went, but not to a tree parking lot where the cost runs between $40 and $80. Nope, we went to one of those big home improvement stores, where an 8 foot Scotch Pine went for a mere $39.99. Can't go wrong with a price like that for a tree that has been dead for a month and has been covered with a fire retardant green paint (just to keep it "green"). It was the deal of the century!

The week after Thanksgiving was a blustery one. I am not a fan of freezing. And anything below 40 degrees is freezing in my book. So, it's needless to say that the 10-minute trek up and down the aisles of the big home improvement store's outside garden area, where countless trees lined the way, was miserable for me.

And then, I saw her. Big, magnificent, full-bodied, not a bald spot anywhere – it was THEE Tree! I called Brian over as I wrestled the beast out from its resting place. We stood her up, twirled her in a circle, slammed her on the ground a few times to make sure no needles fell off, and when we were done with our inspection, I announced that THIS would be our tree.

"What do you think, Bri?" I asked while jumping up and down trying to stay warm.

"She looks good to me. You sure this is the one you want? It's pretty big," he said holding onto the trunk of the tree.

"Yep! This is Thee One. Don't you think so? If you don't like this one, we can keep looking, but we have to do it quickly because body parts are going to start freezing and cracking off."

"I like it. I just want to make sure that you're sure," he smiled as I did my Jack Frost Nipping At My Nose dance.

"Well, I'm sure if you're sure."

Let me break off here for a minute. I find it amazing that one can spend most of their life making decisions without having to take a poll, but when you wind up in a

relationship, everything goes through a process of checks and balances, gives and takes, and finally making a decision without confirmation from the other, is impossible.

Two brains that worked just fine separately, at one time, have somehow assimilated into one. It's actually almost disturbing. But I digress.

So, we hauled our magnificent, large, full-bodied tree to the cash register, paid for the baby, placed her in the back of the pick-up truck, and headed for the farm.

While Brian sawed off a few of the lower branches, I went on a frantic hunt to find the tree stand. I have three of them, but of course, the year before, I put them someplace where I knew I would remember where they were this year, and 365 days later, I had no clue where I had put them. After an hour of climbing around in the rafters of the garage, hanging from my fingertips out of the cubby hole in the attic, digging through closets and boxes of Christmas, I did manage to dig one up, but it wasn't one of the three I knew I had.

I moved the furniture around, put the stand in its place, and called out to Brian that everything was ready!

It took both of us pushing and pulling to get it through the back door, and we could have used a third and fourth person to wrestle the behemoth past the washer and dryer in the utility room, through the kitchen door, and into the living room. I was surprised there were any needles left on the tree when we were done manhandling the poor thing. But, in the twinkling of an eye, Brian had the tree in the stand, I had it secured with those stupid screws (righty tighty, lefty lucy -- I always go the wrong way first), and as soon as I had dug myself out from under the tree and was standing next to Brian, he let go of the trunk and we stepped back in awe of this fine specimen!

She was gorgeous. The perfect tree!

And as we stood, applauding our efforts and our tree pickin' skills -- as the words to Oh Christmas Tree sang in my head -- the tree swayed a little, then bit it! It came down hard, too. Took out the coffee table, and came to rest with a thud that shook the fillings in my teeth.

Silence. I stood on one side of the fallen tree. Brian was on the other. It had split us right down the center.

"What the H..., " I looked over at Brian.

"Wow," was all he said.

So, we got right to work to fix the situation and wrestled her back to an upright position. But before we could step back, the tree came forward again. I wish I could have had someone there to take a picture. I can see the headline: Two people get swallowed alive by demonic Scotch Pine! I was standing next to Brian, but because my head was buried in the branches, all I could see of him was his hand holding, what I now marveled at the most amazingly CROOKED tree trunk I had ever seen. This thing was gnarly. Big time.

And that's when the laughter started.

"OK, so it's NOT the perfect tree," I giggled, "can you see the trunk from where you are?"

A muffled reply came back my way, "Oh yeah... I see it."

"Now what?"

"Well," he said as he leaned the tree against the wall, "now we improvise. I'll be right back."

And off he went to the garage, which is where he does his best thinking and came up with the best plans.

Brian came back with a cinder block, a big rock, a roll of twine, and a knife. And all I could think of was MacGyver -- Why, with those four things, Brian was going to make us a new tree. Was it possible?

We worked together, tying the twine around the cinder block and the rock, then tying the other end of the twine to the trunk of the tree, which, in theory, was done to weigh down the back of the tree and keep it from falling forward. When the work was done. The tree stood tall and straight. I filled the stand with water, and we again applauded our tree pickin' skills and our craftiness. Crooked trunk or not, it was still a beautiful tree.

I drug the box of lights out of the closet (found one of the missing tree stands, top-shelf -- groan) and put them on the tree, ever mindful that I had to be careful. Even though the tree was anchored with a cinder block and a big rock, I didn't want to play with it too much, just in case. After an hour of adjusting the tiny white bulbs and tucking the green cords deep inside the branches, I hit the switch and the room was awash with a warm Christmas glow. It was a masterpiece of grand proportion! No Charlie Brown Christmas here. No way! This tree rivaled Time

Square any day!

We made a delicious dinner of roast beef and tiny potatoes and sat down to enjoy our dinner, and our triumph.

When out in the living room

there arose such a THUD,

I sprang to my feet

mumbling, "Oh Crud".

I slid into the room

on two stocking feet

and wound up in a river of water

about an inch deep.

The whole thing, lights, tree stand, water from the tree stand, oh and lest I forget the possessed tree, lay silent in the night, in the middle of the floor. With mouths agape, we started to laugh. I couldn't help it. I was bummed because we had done all that work, but the fact that we had bought a cursed tree was just too dang funny.

So, we cleaned up the water, leaned the tree back against the wall, repositioned the block and rock, and Brian disappeared out to the garage to do more "thinking".

When he came back inside, he was carrying a long piece of rope, an eye hook, and a stud finder. I didn't ask, I just followed his lead. We found the stud, Brian secured the eye hook and bolted it to the stud, lassoed the tree with the rope, pulled it to the wall, and tied it to the eye hook. The only way this tree was going down again, was if it took the wall with it. Which, is a very real possibility when you live in a farmhouse that is 105 years old.

But, the tree made it through the entire season without falling over again, although I never did take the time to redo the lights. I was afraid to touch that crazy tree. So, the lights just kind of hung where they had landed. As far as ornaments go, those never found their way to the spray-painted branches. Good Lord, all that extra weight?

Not a chance.

In the end, I guess Charlie Brown won, in a manner of speaking. To Brian and I, however, it was the best Christmas Tree ever! Or at the very least, the funniest!

Now, we are off to get this year's tree. After much debate on whether we just wanted to get a fake one with the lights already on it, or go for the real deal again, we decided that a fake one was simply no fun.

We're going to take our chances.

Let the games begin!

Merry Christmas, everyone! May it be magical, and filled with love and laughter!

"Adults can take a simple holiday for Children and screw it up. What began as a presentation of simple gifts to delight and surprise children around the Christmas tree has culminated in a woman unwrapping six shrimp forks from her dog, who drew her name."

– Erma Bombeck

"In the old days, it was not called the Holiday Season; the Christians called it 'Christmas' and went to church; the Jews called it 'Hanukkah' and went to synagogue; the atheists went to parties and drank. People passing each other on the street would say 'Merry Christmas!' or 'Happy Hanukkah!' or (to the atheists) 'Look out for the wall!'"

— Dave Barry

"The office Christmas party is a great opportunity to catch up with people you haven't seen for 20 minutes."

— Julius Sharpe

"A Christmas miracle is when your family doesn't get into a single argument all day."

— Melanie White

The Story Of Slappy Cat Communications LLC

I was nine, and a young budding writer. I knew in my heart of hearts that I had something to offer the literary world. But like all new authors, especially very young authors, no publishing company would give me the time of day.

So, I bought my first newspaper, The Anchor Bay Beacon, at the age of 23, which enabled me to publish my works, and I invited every new writer to join the staff. The paper was filled with authors who just needed a place to start their careers. They, like me, needed a shot, and I gave it to them.

Since that time I have created and published many magazines with new writer's voices front and center.

I've published several of my own books, as well. Being compared as a cross between Dave Barry and Erma Bomback, by my readers, has me doing cartwheels every day.

Slappy Cat Communications LLC was formed in 2011 to house all of the many publications I own, but also to give birth to an Author House, (and marketing division) to publish and market books for authors who can't afford the Self Publishing Industry costs.

My most successful Publication is The Beacon NewsMagazine, which morphed out of the original Anchor Bay Beacon, from November 2, 1991.

What started out as a labor of love, slowly grew into Slappy Cat Communications LLC. My husband, of six years, and I enjoy the creativity of each project we produce for new authors and established authors, alike.

I take pride in what I do here, and will never let any author settle for second best. The book will not go to print until the author is 100% happy.

We look forward to doing business with you in the future.

Thank you!

Sue Ann Veryser-Duncan

Anyone interested in participating in the Summer Anthology 2021 or the Christmas Anthology 2021, please send an email to editor@beaconewsmag.com for all of the information.

Manufactured by Amazon.ca
Bolton, ON